TANGLED UP IN LACE

CHARLOTTE BYRD

ABOUT TANGLED UP IN LACE

Our love isn't like everyone else's. I used to be a recluse, but no more.

She helped me fight my dark past.

Now, it's my turn to help her fight hers.

But she's not here.

I have to find her and show her what I'm willing to do for her.

This is one thing I can't buy.

Am I willing to give up everything to have her?

PRAISE FOR CHARLOTTE BYRD

“Decadent, delicious, & dangerously addictive!” - Amazon Review ★★★★★

“Titillation so masterfully woven, no reader can resist its pull. A MUST-BUY!” - Bobbi Koe, Amazon Review ★★★★★

“Captivating!” - Crystal Jones, Amazon Review ★★★★★

"Exciting, intense, sensual” - Rock, Amazon Reviewer ★★★★★

“Sexy, secretive, pulsating chemistry…” - Mrs. K, Amazon Reviewer ★★★★★

“Charlotte Byrd is a brilliant writer. I've read loads and I've laughed and cried. She writes a balanced book with brilliant characters. Well done!” -Amazon Review ★★★★★

“Fast-paced, dark, addictive, and compelling” - Amazon Reviewer ★★★★★

“Hot, steamy, and a great storyline.” - Christine Reese ★★★★★

“My oh my....Charlotte has made me a fan for life.” - JJ, Amazon Reviewer ★★★★★

"The tension and chemistry is at five alarm level.” - Sharon, Amazon reviewer ★★★★★

“Hot, sexy, intriguing journey of Elli and Mr. Aiden Black. - Robin Langelier ★★★★★

“Wow. Just wow. Charlotte Byrd leaves me speechless and humble... It definitely kept me on the edge of my seat. Once you pick it up, you won't put it down.” - Amazon Review ★★★★★

“Sexy, steamy and captivating!” - Charmaine, Amazon Reviewer ★★★★★

“ Intrigue, lust, and great characters...what more could you ask for?!” - Dragonfly Lady ★★★★★

"An awesome book. Extremely entertaining, captivating and interesting sexy read. I could not put it down." - Kim F, Amazon Reviewer ★★★★★

"Just the absolute best story. Everything I like to read about and more. Such a great story I will read again and again. A keeper!!" - Wendy Ballard ★★★★★

"It had the perfect amount of twists and turns. I instantaneously bonded with the heroine and of course Mr. Black. YUM. It's sexy, it's sassy, it's steamy. It's everything." - Khardine Gray, Bestselling Romance Author ★★★★★

DON'T MISS OUT!

Want to be the first to know about my upcoming sales, new releases and exclusive giveaways?

Sign up for my Newsletter and join my Reader Club!

Bonus Points: Follow me on BookBub!

ALSO BY CHARLOTTE BYRD

All books are available at ALL major retailers! If you can't find it, please email me at charlotte@charlotte-byrd.com

Black Series

Black Edge

Black Rules

Black Bounds

Black Contract

Black Limit

House of York Trilogy

House of York

Crown of York

Throne of York

Standalone Novels

Debt

Offer

Unknown

Dressing Mr. Dalton

PROLOGUE - JACKSON

WHEN THE PAST CRASHES INTO THE PRESENT...

Nostalgia is a mind fuck.

It messes with your head.

It makes you believe things that aren't true.

Sitting here across from Aurora, my ex-wife, I suddenly forget things.

It feels so good to be with her again, so comfortable that the memories of everything bad that happened suddenly floats away and is replaced by everything that is good.

I remember the way her head felt laying in my lap as we read books under a big tree in Central Park that summer when we first met.

I remember the way her hair bounced from side to side as she walked in front of me, holding my hand.

These memories aren't solitary, they are more like a flood.

One memory replaces another and another, leaving me with a general feeling of well-being. She is my past and sometimes it's nice to go back there.

I stare into her eyes. She only looks a bit older than she did back then, but it's her eyes that remain ageless.

They are the same exact ones that I fell for back then.

Aurora wraps her hand around mine and gives me a little squeeze.

There's nothing romantic about it at first, and then...the mood changes.

It's as simple as a look.

One moment she is holding my hand as an old friend, and the next...it's more than that.

I linger in the moment, wrapped in an aura of nostalgia.

She gives me a little smile and reaches up to my face.

She runs her hands up my face and buries them in my hair.

Then she pulls me closer to her.

Our lips are about to touch, but before they do, the past comes crashing into me.

The memories that flood my mind are no longer the nice, comforting ones from the beginning of our relationship.

No, they're the hurt and the pain that came with the end. She is the woman who broke my heart.

I could get over that. I already did. But more importantly, she is the woman who broke my daughter's heart.

When she left me, she also left my daughter.

She left her as a baby never to return.

Being a mother is hard, I understand that.

But she didn't even want to have shared custody.

She didn't want anything to do with her.

I pull away just before our lips touch.

"What's wrong?" Aurora asks.

"I can't do this."

"Oh, c'mon, it's just for a bit of fun."

"I have a girlfriend and even if I didn't...you and I...no."

Aurora shrugs her shoulders and takes another sip of her water.

"You know, it takes some guts to do that," she says, smiling.

"What?"

"Turn me down when I'm the one here trying to save your company."

"That's not something that I even considered," I say. "Listen, let's just forget that ever happened."

"Fine by me."

I can tell that her ego is a bit bruised, but there isn't much else that I can really do.

There was a time when we were first together that I loved her very much.

I thought that my life would end if anything ever happened to us.

But it was a quick burning kind of love.

It was fueled by so much accelerant that it stopped me from seeing how wrong we were for each other.

And just as quickly as it started, it disappeared.

Looking at the woman who is standing before me now, I find it difficult to comprehend that we ever had anything to do with one another.

"I'm sorry that I did that," she says after a moment. "I know you have a girlfriend and...I'm just feeling so shitty."

"Can I ask you something?"

She nods.

"I don't want this to come out as some misogynistic comment or anything like that. And I would ask you this if you were my guy friend."

"Okay..." she says, bracing herself for what's to come.

"But have you ever thought about not jumping from one relationship to another?"

"I'm not jumping from one relationship to another. I'm jumping from one bed to another," she says, crossing her arms. "That's very different."

That's sort of what I meant, but it's not exactly what I wanted to say.

"Look, I know that you are married to a real asshole who treats you like shit. But there are nice guys out there. Really nice ones. Woodward isn't one of them."

"Who is? You?"

"No, I'm not really one of them, either."

She shrugs. "I like men. I like sex. What's wrong with that?"

"Nothing, nothing at all. Except that, it sort of feels like you are searching for something. And I'm not sure you're going to find it doing what you're doing."

Aurora inhales deeply, and for a moment it looks like she's holding back tears.

"What's wrong?" I ask.

"Nothing," she lies.

I don't believe her, but I don't push.

"It's just that recently, I've been thinking a lot about you and me. I think that you might have been the best relationship I've ever been in. And I totally fucked it up."

"Yes, you did," I say.

She looks away.

"Aurora, you fucked it up but you weren't wrong to leave. You were just wrong about how you left."

"What do you mean?"

"We weren't right for each other. I know that now. We had all of these...cracks. There are better people out there for each of us and I know you will find him."

Before I can get all of the words out, I hear a gunshot.

It comes right from outside the front door and Aurora jumps.

I get startled, too, but I remain calm.

"It's probably just a car backfiring," I say. "But I'll go check it out."

When I run out to the stoop, someone's being pushed into a van. A large man is pushing her in against her will. She's shouting. Kicking. Fighting.

"Help!" Her voice cracks as she screams.

"Hey, stop!" I yell, but the man jumps into the van and slides the door shut.

I grab the door handle and try to open it, but the van speeds away.

Without wasting a moment, I fly up the stairs and grab my car keys off the console table in the foyer.

"What are you doing?" Aurora asks. "What's wrong?"

She runs after me to my car, parked just a bit down the block.

"Jackson! What are you doing?"

"Call the cops! Someone took Harley! They forced her into a van. I have to find her."

JACKSON

WHEN I FOLLOW THEM…

The white van turns right at the corner and I follow a few cars behind.

There's a lot of traffic and he can't go that far or that fast.

I dial 911 on my phone and tell them what happened exactly as I saw it.

"What's their license plate?" the operator asks.

His voice is monotone and without much expression, and I wonder if he's bored or just not supposed to get excited because of his job.

"No, I can't see it. I'm following them right now—"

My own voice is rushed and out of control.

I'm actually out of breath as if I'm running.

Suddenly, the operator perks up.

"You're following them?"

"Of course."

"No, please don't do that, sir."

I can't believe what I'm hearing. Is he serious?

"They kidnapped her. No one knows she's in there besides me. I have to follow them."

"That's against policy, sir. Please, leave that to the professionals."

"How the hell are you going to find this van if I can't give you their plate number?"

There's a pause. Instead of answering me, he again pushes me to stop the chase.

"Listen, I'm not going to stop fucking following them. They have my girlfriend. You get that?"

"Sir—" he starts to say, but I cut him off.

"Listen, I'm about a second away from hanging up. Drop it."

"Okay…tell me what's going on. Where are you now?"

We pull up to an intersection and I rattle off the cross streets.

Traffic is winding down.

One car turns left and another turns right.

There's only one car in front of me now, yet I still can't make out the license plate number. Shit.

“C’mon, c’mon, move out of the way,” I say to myself.

“The police will be there soon,” the operator says.

As we come to a stop at a red light, I debate whether I should get out of the car and try to break into their van.

I don’t know how long the light will last and there’s a large SUV in front of me.

If they see me, then they’ll take off and I’ll have to run back to my car.

Despite all of this, I’m itching to go for it.

I wrap my hands so tightly around the steering wheel that my knuckles turn white and then, just as I’m about to reach for the door handle…the van takes off.

“What the fuck?” I step on the gas and swirl around the SUV in front of me.

I veer into oncoming traffic, but luckily that car swerves out of the way.

Surrounded by a cacophony of horns, I chase after the van across the intersection.

But instead of going straight, he suddenly turns left, nearly colliding with a moving truck.

I’m not so lucky.

The truck misses him but runs straight into me.

The world starts to spin and there's nothing I can do to make it stop.

With each rotation, Harley is getting further and further away from me. And then, it all goes black.

WHERE IS SHE?

Why is he doing this?

Where is he taking her?

I don't need the answer to *who* took her.

It's him.

Parker Huntington.

It's the same guy who attacked her on my doorstep.

It's the same guy who crashed her into my life.

It's the same guy who I should've killed right there and then and made the world a better place.

But I didn't.

It's easy to imagine that you would be capable of killing someone in particular circumstances.

We have all watched those movies or television shows where the character hesitates, when we all know that they shouldn't.

Some people think that makes them weak.

But I know better.

That hesitation makes them human.

Because it takes a special kind of inhumanity and callousness to take a life without a second thought.

When Parker first attacked Harley, I didn't know anything about him. I didn't know their history.

I didn't know that he had stalked her and that he was obsessed with this person he thought she was in her writing.

But tonight, I know that I wouldn't hesitate to take him out for a moment.

A man like him doesn't deserve to live.

He is unpredictable and unstable and his obsession is single-minded.

Each contact he has with her makes him more bold, more determined.

To do what exactly?

My body shudders at the thought.

He wants to own her.

She rejected him and he needs to make her his.

I don't know what he wants to do with her but I know that whatever it is isn't good.

I will do everything in my power to stop him.

The only problem is that I don't have much in my power anymore.

My mind isn't clear and my body is broken.

I don't know the details of the damage, but I know the pain that I felt when the truck sideswiped me.

I passed out for a few moments and then woke up here, in the ambulance.

The sirens are deafening and the paramedics are yelling over them.

The world is too much and I can't feel most of my body.

My eyelids feel heavy and impossible to keep open.

"Stay with me, Jackson. Stay with me." The woman puts something plastic and hard over my mouth and fresh oxygen starts to flow into my lungs.

I take a few breaths and my body starts to wake up.

But with this awakening, the pain starts to move through me in waves.

One after another.

And then, one on top of another.

The pain is too much and I close my eyes and fade away.

"We're... losing... him!"

"No...no...no."

JACKSON

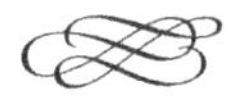

WHEN SHE'S TOO FAR AWAY...

Their voices are faint and far away, consumed by the world full of sirens and screaming and people.

A few more breaths, and I can't hear them anymore.

A few more breaths, and I'm not here at all.

But it is not a long tunnel with white light that welcomes me.

It's a forest with tall pine trees that reach for the blue sky above.

I walk among them, listening to the crunch of the needles under my feet. The sun is high, right above my head, and it blinds me for a moment when I walk out onto the meadow outside.

When my eyes get adjusted, I see her. Harley.

Dressed in a simple white dress, she is sitting on the grass surrounded by a sea of wild flowers.

Her hair, tussled and a bit out of control, falls in waves down her back.

She is staring out into the distance, holding her hand over her eyes to block some of the sun.

I watch as she sits there for a few moments and then lies down.

I want to walk over to her, take her into my arms, but when I make the move, my body levitates and flies above her.

It suddenly dawns on me that she can't see me.

"Harley!" I yell, but she doesn't notice.

All she sees is a shadow that forms over her body.

She looks up at me, unsure as to where the darkness is coming from and then moves a few inches away to continue bathing in the sun.

I yell her name again, but again she doesn't respond.

Why can't I reach her? Why can't she hear me?

With those questions firmly in my mind, I feel myself descending down.

When the ground feels firm and strong under my feet, I sit down.

I am right next to her but she can't hear me.

She can't feel me.

It's as if she's in a glass case, one that makes her impenetrable by me.

"Harley, please, please...say something," I plead.

I place my hand on her shoulder, but she shrugs it off.

Her body shivers and she rubs her shoulder in the place where I touched it, as if my hand was a cold breeze that swept through.

I don't know what to do.

I can't reach her and I don't want to leave.

I want to be here however I can, and if this is it... if this is all I have...then, it will have to be enough.

Right?

Wrong.

I grab her by the shoulder and turn my body toward her.

"Harley, please, you have to see me. I'm here. Right here!" I scream as loud as I can.

Her hair blows back a bit from my force, but she doesn't hear anything. Instead, she wraps her arms around herself and gets up to leave.

"No, no, please don't leave!" I grab her hand but she pulls away. "I'm right in front of you. Please!"

How can someone so real be so far away?

I take my head in my hands and bury it in my

knees. Why can't she see me? Why can't she hear me?

And then...suddenly...it occurs to me. What if?

No, it can't be. I can't even finish the thought in my head. But I have to.

What if...she can't see me because I'm not here?

What if she can't see me because I'm not alive?

What if she can't see me because I'm *dead*?

* * *

I STARE at the meadow trying to figure out the truth.

If I'm dead then I can't be here, thinking these thoughts.

My body wouldn't be here.

And my spirit...I don't believe in that.

I look around again.

A large hawk circles overhead.

Can he see me? I wonder.

My beliefs about life after death...what good are they?

They are just beliefs and now...this...might be my reality.

And if it is?

Then what?

Suddenly a loud beeping sound comes from somewhere all around.

It has no place here, yet it's all I hear.

The beeping sound is followed by loud voices. Arguing.

"You have to keep trying!"

"It's over."

"No, it's not. Do you know who that is?"

"I don't care. Whoever he is, he's dead."

I feel a jolt.

My entire body is lifted off the ground for a moment and then thrown back on.

I close my eyes from impact and when I open them again, all I see is a strong bright white light.

It's blinding.

"Abby, you're beating a dead horse."

"I have to keep trying."

Another jolt lifts me and slams me down.

And then another.

"I'm calling the time of death."

"No, just one more time. Okay?"

The last jolt feels different than the rest.

It slams me into the ground, making a faint ticking sound start up somewhere in the distance.

"I've got a heartbeat!" an excited voice says.

A smell of something burning permeates into my

nostrils mixed with other smells of cleaning products and soap.

I try to open my eyes, but my eyelids are too heavy to lift. Instead, I listen as a large group of people start to gather around me.

They are all talking at once, making it difficult to make out what anyone is saying.

"Jackson? Can you see me?" a woman in her mid-forties asks me.

I recognize her voice immediately.

She was the one who refused to call the time of death.

I nod and try to talk, but there's something in my mouth.

Someone removes the breathing tube, scratching my throat. I cough until it feels better.

"Where's Harley?"

HARLEY

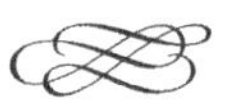

WHEN THEY TAKE ME…

His breathing makes me sick to my stomach. It's quick and labored.

I can smell his breath from here, a nauseating mixture of something that doesn't go together like garlic and chocolate.

I need to get out of here but how?

My hands are tied in the front and there's a blindfold over my eyes.

The man next to me wheezes as he inhales and he's sitting only a few feet away, looking at me.

Where did Parker find him?

And who the hell would agree to commit a kidnapping?

It's a federal crime, right? It's at least a state crime.

My fear is starting to get the best of me and shivers start to crawl up my skin. No, you need to focus.

Don't let them win.

Just focus on memorizing any details.

I say the words over and over again until I start to believe myself.

Yes, that is what I need to do.

Focusing on the fear isn't going to help me, but this will.

The guy who forced me into the van has bad breath, but besides that he is also heavy with a large gut.

He is surprisingly firm on his feet and strong, but his hair is thinning and long.

He's balding a bit on top, but has his long hair pulled up in a stringy ponytail.

Not the best look.

How old is he?

Based on his weight and look, probably well into middle age. But I can't narrow it down any more than that.

It all happened so fast that I can't even really remember details about his face. What I do remember is the sound of the gun shot going off next to me on the pavement.

And the fear that rushed through me at that moment.

I take a deep breath to gather my strength.

"Where are you taking me?" I ask.

"Shut the fuck up," the man next to me hisses, depositing a few drops of spit on my face.

I recoil in fear.

My heart is beating out of my chest, as if it's about to jump out. In a state of shock, the body tends to shut down.

People wonder why some people facing an execution stand motionless and don't even try to run or protest.

But it happens because every part of you shuts down.

I've experienced that before.

When Parker showed up places I was supposed to be and made threats, I just stopped in my tracks and listened, not because I wanted to hear what he was saying but because I couldn't physically make my body move.

It's happening again.

It feels like every cell in my body is being depleted of energy.

The only thing I can do is sit here and tremble.

I see this happening to me in third person.

It's as if my spirit leaves the rest of me here, tied up and blindfolded, and watches from above.

No, no, no. I say to myself.

"No," I mutter under my breath.

If I shut down then they win.

I have to fight.

The first fight will be internal.

I will not let myself shut down. I know what it feels like to feel powerless, but I am not. I may not have any physical power right now, but I do have internal power.

I have the power to control my thoughts. I have the power to control how I interpret and feel about this situation.

And this power is strong.

No matter what they do to me, they cannot take it away.

"Where are you taking me?" I ask again.

This time my voice is stronger.

I am no longer asking a question. I am demanding an answer.

"What did I say?" The man next to me shoves me into the wall of the van.

"Parker Huntington...tell me."

No one says anything for a few moments.

I've made an impact.

What kind of impact I'm not entirely sure, but I suspect that the other kidnapper doesn't like the fact that I know Parker's name.

"How do you know who he is? How does she know who you are?" he asks.

I can hear the panic in his voice and a small smile forms at the corner of my lips.

I don't know how much he can see, so I make it go away as quickly as possible.

He climbs over me to the front of the van. "Tell me!"

"She knows me, so what?" Parker asks.

Finally, I have confirmation that it is he who is behind this.

I've known it all along, but this is the first time that I know it for sure.

"It's a big fucking deal, that's what. You told me that you just had an eye on her, not that she knew you, too."

I see an opening.

"Did Parker tell you that he also attacked me before? That he was arrested and he's currently out on bail and awaiting trial for that crime?"

"What the fuck?" The man gasps.

"He's going to be the first person they will suspect."

"Don't listen to her," Parker says. "It's all going to be fine."

"How, how's it going to be fine?" the man asks.

He's freaking out. I've done my job in creating a fracture in between them. Now, I have to break them apart for good.

"I know who he is, but I don't know who you are. And if you help me, then no one ever has to know."

I wait for him to respond.

"What do you mean?"

"Help me get out of here. Just let me out and I won't tell them you that you were involved."

"Yeah, right," Parker says.

"Yes. Right," I insist. "How can I? I don't know your name and I don't know anything about you."

"Don't believe her, Sam. She knows what you look like."

"Fuck, Parker! Why did you have to tell her my name?"

My throat closes up.

That's the last thing I want to know. I have a feeling that he might go for this, but if I know his name then...My thoughts trail off as my hope starts to diminish.

"It doesn't matter," I insist. "That doesn't matter.

Please, you have to help me. I won't tell anyone about you."

"You lied to me, Parker," Sam says. His voice sounds exasperated and tired.

Please, please, please, believe me, I pray silently to myself. You have to believe me.

"I don't want to do this anymore," Sam says.

"That's too damn bad. You're in this."

Parker is confident and determined, so much unlike the man that I first met who was too scared to even talk to me. How the hell did he morph into this...*monster*?

"Pull over," Sam says. "I don't want to be a part of this anymore."

"Don't believe her!"

"Pull over!"

HARLEY

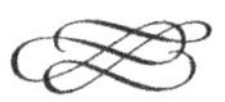

WHEN THEY TAKE ME...

I raise my hands to Sam and whisper, "Untie me, please untie me."

"I'm not pulling over. Besides, this is your van. I'm going through with the plan."

"I don't want to be here anymore. You lied to me."

"Of course I lied to you, you wouldn't let me use your van if I hadn't."

"You have to make him stop," I whisper under my breath.

"What? What are you saying back there?" Parker asks.

I don't repeat myself.

"Pull over, Parker!" Sam yells.

"No! She's lying, Sam, can't you see that?" Parker

insists. "Harley, since you know my name, why don't we even the playing field a bit, huh?"

"Don't you fucking do it!" Sam reaches over to the driver's seat.

All I hear is a scuffle and then the van starts to swerve from one side of the street to the other.

I bring my hands up to my face and move the blindfold out of the way.

I haven't done it until now because I didn't want to see what Sam looked like just in case I could convince him to let me go.

With the blindfold propped up just a bit, I bring my hands to my mouth and try to untie them.

But the knot is too strong.

I glance over at the front and see Sam grabbing the wheel and Parker trying desperately to hang onto it.

I brace myself against the wall and wait for the crash.

"His name is Samual Donald Davis. He was born and raised in Queens. He is fifty-one years old. He is a delivery driver. I met him at a coffee shop in the Village."

As Parker rattles off everything he knows about Sam, Sam yells for him to stop.

He shouts and punches him, but the words keep coming.

My heart drops as I hear each new piece of information as my fate is being sealed.

"He works for a florist," Parker finally says when Sam pulls away from him in defeat.

The van comes to a slow stop and we are no longer weaving from one lane to another.

I pull my blindfold back down, leaving a little slit through which I can see right over the bridge of my nose.

I watch as Sam sits back in the front seat, defeated.

"Why did you tell her all of that?" he finally asks.

Parker adjusts his shirt and repositions himself confidently in the driver's seat.

"For your own good. You were concerned that she knew too much about me. Well, now she knows everything about you as well."

I debate whether I should speak up again and continue to plead for Sam to help me. But something stops me. That fight is lost, and perhaps it's best to just keep quiet for now.

"Listen, whatever she knows or she doesn't know, isn't going to matter. She's ours now. You get that?"

A cold shiver runs through me. What the hell does that mean?

"We just need to stick to our plan, that's it. Nothing bad is going to happen then."

Parker is swaying him now. His voice is calm and soothing, and his approach is working. Sam nods and relaxes a bit.

"Besides, now that she knows a bit about us, why don't I tell you a bit about her."

My jaw clenches in anger and I again try to gnaw at the restraints around my wrists.

Parker begins to tell Sam about who he thinks I am.

He tells him about my blog and about all the dirty things that he thinks I did.

He tells him about how he first fell in love with my words and then he had to go find me.

He talks about me as if I'm not here and after a few minutes they seem to both forget about me.

As he speaks, I bury myself in the dark corner right behind the driver's seat, where I am a bit out of sight, and continue to pick at my bindings.

"You really did all those things?" Sam turns to me suddenly. I freeze in place but notice that he doesn't turn around.

“I didn’t do any of those things,” I say. “I’m a writer. It was a made up blog.”

“Please.” Parker shakes his head. “You really expect me to believe that you didn’t do any of those things.”

“No, I didn’t.”

“Then you have one hell of an imagination.”

"Yeah, I guess I do.”

“Don’t believe her,” Parker says. “She’s the girl. She’s the slut. And now, she’s ours.”

I clench my fists in anger. Who does he think he is? And even if I did do those things, even if I were an escort, so what? That’s my right. And it’s not his right to stalk me, or terrorize me, or kidnap me.

“Sam, you don’t have to do this,” I plead. “He’s lying.”

“You didn’t have a blog?”

“I did, but so what? It was just for fun. I’m a writer. I make things up.”

“You are one fucked up writer.” Parker laughs. “If you can make those things up then...that’s pretty much the same as doing them.”

“No, it’s not! But in either case...you have no right to...take me.”

“Well, that’s the kind of man I am now. I take what I want. I didn’t always do that and women just laughed at me. They thought that I was a joke. You were one of those women. Well, no more."

So, that's why he's doing this. He got rejected a few too many times and now he's taking it out on me. Of course, I say to myself.

My mind races as I try to think of some way to respond.

"Is that why you're doing this, Sam? Is that why you're helping him? Is it worth spending the rest of your life in prison just so Parker can 'take what's his'?"

I watch him think about that for a moment and let out a small sigh. At least, my words are making an impact. Perhaps then...I can get him on my side.

"No, it's not," Sam eventually mumbles.

"What are you getting out of this, Sam? Why are you helping him? If you help me then I'll make it worthwhile."

"How?"

"Don't listen to her!" Parker roars.

"What are you going to do, Harley? You going to not tell the police who I am?"

"No, I won't," I promise.

"Yeah, right."

"Yes, right," I insist. Please, please believe me, I add silently.

"Of course, she's going to tell them. What reason would she have to keep quiet once she's free? You can't trust her, Sam."

"Sam, please," I insist. "You're a good person. I know that. You don't want to do this."

Sam doesn't say anything for a bit as Parker and I go back and forth trying to influence his decision.

"I am a good person," Sam finally says. I let out a sigh of relief. He believes me. Everything is going to be okay. He's going to take my side.

"But it's too late for you. I can't trust you. You know too much."

HARLEY

WHEN I RAGE...

My heart sinks into the pit of my stomach. Whatever progress I thought I was making dissipates and vanishes in a moment. Somewhere in the background, I hear Parker laughing quietly.

Don't give up, I say to myself. This isn't over until it's over. As my hope starts to diminish, I inhale deeply and try to focus my mind. How does that saying go again? Eighty-five percent of success is just showing up. In anything. Convincing Sam didn't work, but something else will. I have to keep trying until...until what? One deep breath follows another. I have to keep trying until. That's it. That's the end of the sentence. I do it until.

No one knows that I'm here and all I have is

myself and my wits to depend on. I will not die at the hands of these assholes. I will not let them kill me. I will not bend. I will not give up hope.

As the van continues to drive further and further into the unknown, taking me away from everything that I am and that I love, I take myself to one of my favorite poems. It's by Dylan Thomas and I first heard it in Dangerous Minds, a 90s movie with Michelle Pfeiffer. I loved it so much that I wrote it over and over again in my notebook until I knew the words by heart.

Peering into the darkness in front of me, I start to recite my favorite parts silently to myself.

Though wise men at their end know dark is right,
Because their words had forked no lightning they
Do not go gentle into that good night.

Grave men, near death, who see with blinding sight
Blind eyes could blaze like meteors and be gay,
Rage, rage against the dying of the light.

The van slows down and comes to a stop. My heart

jumps but I focus on my meditation. It's like the words are infusing me with the strength to fight.

"Do not go gentle into that good night," I repeat to myself over and over again. 'Rage, rage against the dying of the light.'

We make a turn onto something other than a street. A parking lot, perhaps. Then we come to a stop and Parker turns off the engine.

"Rage, rage against the dying of the light," I yell to myself in complete silence.

Sam gets out and slides the door to the back open. When he reaches for me, I lean back and kick him as hard as I can with both feet. Surprised, he bounces away from me and falls on his back.

I pull my blindfold off and start running.

They took me to some empty parking lot in front of a warehouse, but I don't stop to look around much. Once I clear the entrance, I turn right down a deserted city street. We've driven for a while, but we are probably somewhere still in New York City. Definitely in one of the boroughs. Sam is from Queens so we might be there.

When my stomach gets a cramp in it, I don't slow down a bit.

"Rage, rage against the dying of the light," I repeat to myself over and over again. It's my mantra now. The words that keep me going through the pain.

I glance over my shoulder once or twice and don't see anyone following me. Did I really get away?

Not yet. They're still not far behind. I need somewhere to hide. I look around as I run, but the street is full of warehouses and empty lots. There are many places to hide, but I'm too scared to pick the wrong one.

They are still too close to me and if I were to hide now, then they might find me. No, I should keep going. Keep trying to get as far away as possible from them.

Suddenly, I get worried that I've been on this one street too long. They're probably following me and it's too deserted here to hide. I turn right at the next intersection and that's when he grabs me.

Bam!

Sam collides into me and grabs on, hard.

"Where the fuck do you think you're going?" He laughs and pushes me down to the ground. His grasp is firm and strong. When he pushes my face into the pavement, the rocks and debris from the street make their way into my mouth, leaving it with the taste of motor oil.

I try to break free, but he presses his whole body on top of mine and I can't budge an inch.

"You owe me, you bitch," he huffs. "You made me run and I hate running."

"Fuck you," I mumble into the pavement. He doesn't hear me so he lifts my head up by my ponytail and asks me to repeat myself.

"Fuck you!"

Something hard hits the back of my head and everything goes black.

I don't know how long I've been out, but when I wake up I find myself in the back of a sedan with a bag over my head. Sam is sitting next to me, petting my thighs.

Cold shivers run down my spine at his touch. I know what he wants and it makes me sick to my stomach.

"You shouldn't have run, Harley," Parker says from the driver's seat.

"Oh, yeah, why not? Would my fate be any different?" I ask with anger rising out of me.

"Hmm...I guess you're right. Still, it wasn't a nice thing to do."

"This isn't a nice thing to do."

"This is necessary, Harley. I asked you out nicely

many times before. And you said no. What the hell was I supposed to do?"

"Take no for an answer."

He starts to laugh. "I don't do that anymore, Harley. Now, I take what I want."

HARLEY

WHEN THEY TAKE ME THERE...

With each passing minute, we leave more and more of the city behind us. There are not so many stops now. We get onto a highway and pick up speed. I don't know where we're going except that we're going away. Eventually, we take an exit and start driving up a winding rural road. I can see a little bit through the sack on my head, but I can't see much of significance. Everything is black.

Finally, another car passes us. Their headlights illuminate the road and show the tall trees towering along each side. Most of them are leafless, standing stark naked against the elements. The car makes another right turn and finally comes to a stop.

"Where are we?"

"Home," Parker says in a low, menacing voice. Goose bumps form on the back of my arms.

"Take off her shoes," he adds.

"What? Why? No!" I start to resist and kick him when he tries to get my shoes.

"Hold her," Parker says and opens the door. Sam holds me by my hands as I kick at Parker.

Suddenly, he pulls out a gun and puts it in my face.

"You either stop fighting or I'll blow a hole through your foot."

The way he says it and the detail that he uses convinces me that I shouldn't keep struggling. I let my body go limp as Parker pulls off my ankle boots and places them in the back of the trunk.

"Now, get out," he says, waving the gun again. I do as he says.

It's probably around ten degrees outside and the ground is frozen solid. It snowed not too long ago, and my feet recoil with each step. The shoes are a precaution so that I don't run away again. I get it now.

This kidnapping is a lot more planned out than I had previously thought.

Sam leads me down a path full or rocks and debris toward a cabin. I don't want to go in there, but

I don't dare make a move. I wouldn't get too far in my bare feet. I can see only a little bit in front of me through the sack on my head until we get inside.

Then he pulls it off, revealing a knotty pine one bedroom cabin with low ceilings and a small wood-burning fireplace in the middle of the room. The cabin isn't exactly warm, just warmer than the outside.

"Go get the wood," Parker says and Sam leaves us alone.

I continue standing right where he left me until Parker tells me to sit down.

The couch is made of velvet and makes a loud crinkling sound under my butt. My socks are wet from the melting snow and I pull them off and start to warm up my feet.

"You really gave me a scare back there," Parker says, reclining in the large leather chair to the side of the couch.

"What do you mean?"

"By running away. I thought that was it for sure."

I shrug, not sure what I should say in response. I wished that was it.

Parker's face contorts as he smiles and looks me up and down. I can feel that he has been waiting for this moment for a very long time. Perhaps even since he first met me. Was this his plan all along? If I had gone on that date with him, was he planning on kidnapping me? Or maybe, he would've just left me alone. Maybe he would've realized that we don't really have anything in common and that there's someone else out there for him.

Somehow, I doubt that.

I don't know much about him personally, but I suspect that he's the type of man who lives almost entirely in his head. He doesn't socialize much and his perceptions of reality rule his perception of everyone around him. Most people are like that, but only the really crazy ones live in a reality that is completely devoid of what life is really like. And only the really crazy ones would allow themselves to kidnap someone and hold them against their will.

"So, what's your plan?" I ask. "What do you want from me?"

Parker is surprised by my question. He looks as if this part has never occurred to him. Sam comes back into the cabin, holding chopped wood. He kneels down next to the fireplace and starts arranging the kindling.

"When you imagined how this would go, when you planned it all out and got Sam involved, what did you think was going to happen now? When you got me here?"

Parker shakes his head.

"You didn't think that far ahead?" I ask. I am picking at him, trying to get a rise. I'm not entirely sure why except that it feels like the right thing to do. Maybe if I act domineering, then he'll think I'm more powerful than I really am. Maybe then he'll start to second-guess himself.

"Of course, I did," he finally says, catching me off guard.

"Eh, I guess this is as good a time as ever," he says, getting up and going to the closet. Sam looks up at him surprised. My heart sinks. What have I done?

He pulls something out of the closet and hands it to me. It takes me a moment to process what it is I'm looking at.

"Change into that," he says.

I get up and take the garment bag by the plastic hanger.

"You can use the bedroom back there."

I let out a small sigh of relief. For a second, I thought that I would have to change right here.

"Don't think about doing anything stupid in there," Parker says. "And don't close the door."

I do as he says. I walk into the room and look at the queen bed with the winter themed comforter on top. There are two small nightstands on either side and a dresser across from it. The room has a window, but I know better than to try to see if it's locked. They are both staring right at me. I need to build up their trust before I can try to run away again. Also, I need shoes.

I look down at the garment bag in my hand. I can't see through it and I hold my breath as I pull down the zipper. What I find inside catches me by surprise.

I don't know what I was expecting but it was definitely not…this.

"Are you changing? I don't hear you changing!" Parker yells from the other room.

I take a few steps away from the door for some privacy and take off my top. I pull the white turtle neck over my head and then put on the vest. I take off my pants and pull up the pleated skirt. It's short but not too short. Finally, I put on the vest. I glance at myself in the mirror.

I'm a fucking *cheerleader*!

HARLEY

WHEN THEY TAKE ME THERE...

I come out of the room slowly, straightening my skirt.

"Whoa," Sam says. "Why the hell are you wearing that?"

I shrug.

"You look...perfect," Parker says, taking a few steps toward me. He touches the hem of my skirt and runs his fingers up my body. I flinch but he doesn't actually touch me.

Then he goes to his bag and pulls out two pom-poms, which are a perfect match to the canary color of the skirt. The skirt and the vest are both dark blue with stripes of yellow and white. I take the pom-poms and then tilt my hip and bring them to my sides.

"That's...exactly how I imagined it!" Parker exclaims. There's a kind of innocence in his voice, something that I never expected. I don't know where it's coming from and it catches me by surprise.

"I don't know any cheers."

"That's okay. You'll learn."

My heart falls. Not so innocent after all.

"Why do you want her to wear that?" Sam asks, once he gets the fire going.

The room starts to heat up and blood finally starts to circulate around my body. As far as mandatory outfits go, this one isn't too bad. I am wearing a turtle neck and sleeves down to my wrists. At least, it's not lingerie or a see through dress.

"Sydney Black," Parker says. I furrow my brows.

"Who's that?" Sam asks.

"Sydney Black was the girl of my dreams in ninth grade. She was the head cheerleader at our school. A junior!"

Wow, this explains so much, I think to myself.

"Was she your girlfriend or something?"

"I wish." Parker laughs and then gives out a little snort. "No, she was just someone I knew. All too briefly."

"What happened to her?" I ask.

"She died. Sydney Black died, can you believe

that? I mean, how the hell are we all still alive and she's dead?"

I don't know how to even begin answering that question.

"So...is that what this is about?" I ask. "You want me to be...her?"

"No, of course not!" he says quickly. His voice cracks a bit as he looks away. "You could never be her."

I make a decision to not push the matter anymore.

Sam changes the topic by struggling to make a roaring fire and gets into an argument with Parker about the best way to make bigger flames. I take a seat on the window ledge and wait. Grateful for the time that I have to figure out my next plan of action.

Darkness surrounds us and it will only be a matter of time before it will be time for bed. What's going to happen then? My blood runs cold at the thought. Will he leave me alone or will he finally make his move? And what do I do in return? Do I fight him even though I have a very small chance of fighting him off? Or do I just lay there and wait for it to be over?

My thoughts drift to Jackson. I plead for him to come find me, even though I know that it's probably useless. He has no idea that I was anywhere near his house when this happened. He has no idea that I'm missing at all. No one does. Julie thinks that I'm spending the night with Jackson and Jackson is probably spending the night with that woman with the high cheekbones and impossibly glossy hair. Who the hell is she? And why was she touching him like that?

All of these thoughts flood my mind all at once. I am at once terrified, jealous, angry, and questioning.

Yet, despite all that, I keep going back to him. Jackson. I want to know who that woman was, but not as much as I want him to come and save me. Find me. Look for me. I focus my mind on him, trying desperately to will him to do this across space and time. But it's all useless. I know that. Even if he does feel like something is wrong, he probably won't pay attention to it. I mean, who would? It's just a feeling. Besides, I'm not really missing. Not according to any police report. Absolutely no one knows that I'm here.

Well, except these two.

I glance over at Parker and Sam enjoying beers in front of a television screen. When the show comes to an end, Parker finishes his bottle and gets up.

Stretching his hands above his head, he yawns really loud and then coughs to clear his throat.

"Well, I'm going to head to bed now. Sam, you take the couch."

My heart jumps into my throat.

"You going to the bedroom?" Sam asks.

Parker nods. I clench my fists.

"C'mon, Harley. You're sleeping with me."

JACKSON

WHEN THEY WON'T TELL ME…

Hours in the hospital pass slowly. It's as if time stands still in a place of white walls and sterile floors and people who keep shuffling in and out of your room at all hours of the day and night. By all accounts, I am lucky to be alive. Not only did I make it out of the accident with a truck without any major injuries, I also lucked out because I had a doctor like Abby Langston who refused to call the time of death and kept trying to restart my heart.

I glance at the clock. I woke up nearly four hours ago and I still don't know anything about Harley. I keep asking about her but the nurses just keep saying that they don't know. I believed them at first, but now I'm not so sure. They are avoiding eye contact with me as if they know something.

"So, how are you feeling?" Dr. Langston stops by, picking up my chart.

"Fine."

"Now, I doubt that," she says with a smile.

My head is pounding and my shoulder is throbbing. I haven't seen my face yet, but there are bandages all around. Despite the pain, I force myself to sit up.

"Please, don't move—," she starts to say.

"Dr. Langston, please tell me what's going on."

"Well, the accident caused a lot of trauma, but luckily none of them are life threatening —"

"No, not about that," I cut her off. "About Harley."

"I really don't know anything about that," she says, looking away for a moment. But the way she turns her pale, tired face away from me makes me suspect that she's not really telling me the truth.

"I can handle it. Please, whatever it is, I just have to know," I say. It's a lie. A boldface lie. If she were to tell me that Harley is dead...there's no way I could handle that. But I do need to know. Something. Anything.

"The police will be here soon," she says after a moment. "They want to speak with you."

"Please, tell me."

She closes the chart and looks at me. "I don't know anything. Just some rumors."

Ah! Yes. Finally.

"That's enough. That's all I need."

But she turns to walk away.

"Where are you going?"

"The police need to speak to you first," she says, walking out of the door.

Agh! I want to scream. I grab hold of the rail on the bed and shake it as hard as I can. It doesn't move. I try to pull myself up and climb out, but my body is too weak. Moving just an inch sends impulses of pain through every bit of me.

After a few moments, I give up and lie back in the bed. Helpless. Hopeless. Alone.

Being alone was never a problem before. I spent years wandering around my mansion, completely at peace with never seeing another soul. But then I wasn't helpless. My body was strong and so was my spirit. I've never experienced anything like this before.

Lying here in this hospital bed, dependent on strangers for every little thing, I hate it. I haven't been awake for that long and I already can't stand every part of my new life.

This isn't going to last forever, I say to myself. Every hour I will get stronger. And maybe in a few days, I can get out of here. But with my head pounding so hard that it feels like it's about to explode, it's impossible to place myself anywhere but here.

With a button on the bed, I dim the lights and close my eyes. I don't want to see myself in this bed, trapped in this hospital. I want to be somewhere else. I want to be some place where I'm strong and powerful and the man that I used to be. But mostly, I want to be with Harley.

In the dark, surrounded by the beeping of various monitors, my thoughts drift back to her. My sweet Harley. I should have never let her walk out. I should've fought for her harder. When she told me to go away, I should've stayed.

I wrote her letters, yes, but were they enough? I'm not a writer. How could I think that they would convey enough of how I truly feel? And what if she never read them at all? What if she simply tossed them in the trash?

My world becomes full of regrets. They swirl around me, grab onto me, and pull me down into an abyss as if they were anchors. There are so many things that I would do differently now. So many things that I should've done differently then. I know that. But what use is it to know these things? What does it matter if I can't change anything?

And now...she's gone. They took her. And I couldn't stop them. I should've walked out the door when I first heard the commotion. I shouldn't have waited until the gun shot. I should've *known* that she was out there.

"Hey!" Aurora runs in and throws herself over me. Her body feels warm and comforting draped over mine. When she finally pulls away, she kisses my cheeks over and over again until I ask her to stop. There are tears in her eyes.

"I thought that you weren't going to make it," she whispers.

"I'm fine."

"How are you, really?"

"As good as can be expected, I guess. I can't really move and my head is pounding."

"Dr. Langston says you were really lucky."

"Yeah, that's what people keep saying."

Aurora sits up and stares at me. "You should be really grateful."

"For what?"

"That you aren't dead. Or paralyzed or in a coma," she says sternly.

I know that she's right, but I don't really feel very grateful right now. Still, I don't want to fight.

"Yeah, you're right," I say after a moment.

"What's wrong?" Aurora asks, narrowing her eyes.

"I need to know what happened to Harley."

JACKSON

WHEN I LEARN THE TRUTH…

Aurora flips on the lights and glares at me.

"Why the hell did you do that?" I ask, raising my hand over my eyes. The bright lights flare up my migraine and I start to see lights.

"Because you're an asshole, Jackson. I've been worried sick about you all this time and she's all you care about."

I shake my head and apologize; what else can I do?

"She's not all I care about, I'm glad you're here. And I'm glad that I'm going to be okay. But she got kidnapped, Aurora, and no one wants to tell me anything about it."

She walks over to the window, shaking her head.

"Do you know what's going on?"

"The cops are coming to talk to you."

"Yes, I know, Dr. Langston told me."

"They'll tell you then."

Her words give me pause. It sounds like she knows something and refuses to tell me.

"What do you know, Aurora?"

"Why don't you just wait for the cops?"

"What do you *fucking* know?" I raise my voice.

"Don't yell at me!"

"If you're not going to tell me then get the fuck out of my room," I say sternly.

She walks over to my bed and sits down on the chair next to it. Brushing her hair behind her ears, she looks directly into my eyes. I wait.

"They got away. They found the van, but they must've switched cars. No one knows where they are."

Her words are slow and deliberate. She watches my reaction at each one, but I don't react. I freeze and my face goes flat. Expressionless.

"Did you hear me?" she asks.

I nod.

"Are you okay?"

I nod.

I can't lie. A part of me is relieved. The way that people were avoiding my questions, my mind went somewhere worse. A part of me thought that she was dead and they had found her body. But she's not. She's not here, but she's not dead. And that means that there's still hope.

"Do they have any leads?" I ask.

Aurora shrugs her shoulders.

There's a knock on the door.

A woman comes in dressed in a leather jacket and black pants. She shows me her badge and introduces herself as Detective Richardson. After asking me how I'm feeling, she asks me to go over everything that happened that night up to the accident. I give her all the details that I can remember, up to the point of the accident.

"The last thing I remember is how the van just took off on a red light."

"You don't remember the truck hitting you?"

I shake my head.

"That's not unusual."

"Where's Harley?"

Detective Richardson takes a deep breath. "She's...missing."

"Missing?"

"We don't know. We found the van in a warehouse and we've run prints. The only fingerprints we found inside belong to her."

"Who does the van belong to?"

"A man named Samual Donald Davis from Queens. Fifty-one years old. He's a delivery driver for a floral shop."

I'm glad to hear that they have some information, but I don't really know what to do with it.

"What does that mean?" I ask.

"Well, he hasn't shown up to work. We've dispatched police officers to his home and he isn't there either. There's a good chance he's involved."

I nod.

"What about Parker? Her stalker?"

Detective Richardson gives out a long sigh.

"We haven't been able to locate him either. He's out on bail but he's not home or at work."

I feel myself getting anxious and impatient.

"He's behind this, you know that, right?"

"He is our number one suspect."

I nod. She doesn't continue.

"So...what are you doing about it?"

"We're doing everything we can, Mr. Ludlow."

"Which is?"

"Searching for Harley."

"But what does that mean exactly?"

"I can't disclose much more than this, and

frankly I probably shouldn't have told you this much."

"Detective, please...you have to do something."

She puts her hand over mine.

"I know that you are scared, but we are doing the best we can. The problem is that we don't know what car they switched to after the van. We don't know where they are or where they were even heading."

My heart drops. They don't know anything. They don't have any leads.

"They could be out of the state by now," I whisper. "Or out of the country."

"That's not likely because neither Mr. Huntington or Mr. Davis have passports."

"They could have them under other names."

"It's possible." She shrugs. "But Harley doesn't have a passport. And to take her out of the country, they would have to sneak her out. It is highly unlikely."

"So, what is likely?" I ask, getting more and more impatient.

"Why don't you tell me a little more about what happened that night? Anything else you can remember?"

I demand to know more, but she brushes me off again. She wants to hear my story again. And again.

I comply, thinking that afterward she'll tell more about Harley. But she doesn't. Instead, she says that she will be in touch.

"What the fuck was that?" I ask Aurora after Detective Richardson leaves.

"What do you mean?"

"It's like they don't think this is a big deal. I mean, does this happen all the time or something?"

"They do think it's a big deal, Jackson. They're doing everything they can."

"But how do you know that?"

"Because...they are," she says, shrugging her shoulders.

"No, we need to do more."

She stares at me.

"We need to hire a private detective. A team of private detectives. Richardson probably has other cases. But these people won't. They'll work on this around the clock."

"Jackson, you need to relax. You are getting too excited and it's not good for your health."

My mind is racing a mile a minute. Even my migraine seems to have subsided a bit to make room for all of my thoughts.

"Where are my things?" I ask.

"You can't leave!" She freaks out.

"No, I just need my phone," I explain. "Please, can you find it?"

She looks around the room and checks the closet.

"I don't think you have any things. I know they had to cut your clothes off you in the ambulance."

"Okay, let me have yours then."

She hands it to me reluctantly. "Who are you going to call?"

"Harley's mother."

JACKSON

WHEN I CALL THEM...

As I log into my cloud account to access my contact list through Aurora's phone, she asks me a million questions about what I'm doing. I answer them as best as I can. I have Harley's father's phone number in my phone and I need to tell him what's going on. He has the right to know as her father, but this isn't a courtesy call. Her mother is a lieutenant in the Montana Highway Patrol and though it's not the same jurisdiction, I know that having her here will have an impact on the investigation.

Aurora watches me as I dial and talk. I try to be as clear as possible, even as I hear the panic rising in Harold's voice.

"What's wrong?" I hear someone ask on the

other line. It's Leslie, her mother. Harold puts me on speaker phone and repeats everything that I told him. The words come out flat and emotionless. Is it because I'm in shock? For some reason whatever anxiety or panic I felt earlier has become buried deep within me.

They ask me more and more questions. As soon as Leslie gets on the line, she takes charge. Her policewoman voice appears and she sounds exactly like Detective Richardson. Determined. Reserved.

Harold, on the other hand, doesn't handle it as well. I even hear sobs.

"Is there anything else that you haven't told us yet?" Leslie asks.

"No, that's it."

"Thank you for calling. We really appreciate it."

I feel like she's about to hang up on me, so I stop her.

"I'm going to reach out to a private detective. I don't think the cops are doing enough. Or maybe they're just busy. Anyway, I want more people searching for her."

"That's a good idea. And we will be there as soon as we can."

I smile. That's exactly what I wanted to hear.

"I'm already looking at flights," Harold says, clicking on his computer.

"Oh, there's no need for that. I'll get you a private plane."

After a long pause that makes me think that I had said something wrong, Leslie finally says, "Thank you. Just let us know the details."

LESLIE AND HAROLD BURKE arrive in my hospital room later that evening. They have already met with the cops and Detective Richardson and they look tired but energized. Unlike the people I met in that hospital waiting room before, they seem completely different. Instead of two people, they are a couple. They lean on each other for support and they give each other glances that only they know the meaning of.

After Harold asks me how I am feeling, Leslie gets straight to the point. She's in her element. She is confident and put together and assertive. She is the one who asks all the questions and the one that explains whatever needs to be explained to Harold. We go over what we know so far. I relate what Richardson told me and she confirms the details.

"The private detective should be here tomorrow morning. We hired the one that had the best recommendations."

"We?"

Oh, yes, I completely forgot. Aurora left to get some rest after spending the day with me.

"Aurora, my ex-wife. She's staying with me for a bit. She was there with me when it happened."

Leslie nods without much of an expression, but Harold glares at me.

"She's staying with you? Does Harley know?"

I don't want to go into the details right now, but I'm not sure if I have a choice.

"She's married. She's going through something with her husband. You don't have anything to worry about," I insist.

I decide not to mention the fight or anything related to it. But it still doesn't seem enough for Harold. Leslie, on the other hand, doesn't give it another thought.

"Was she there that night?" she asks after a moment. I nod. "I'd like to speak with her tomorrow." I nod again.

They stay for close to two hours. We don't talk about much besides Harley and I go over my story again and again until Leslie is satisfied. What is it with police officers and wanting to hear the same story over and over again? Is it that they think they're going to catch the person talking in a lie? Perhaps. At least, according to the crime shows on television. But I get the feeling that she's looking for something else as well. An inconsistency. And perhaps, even a super-consistency. You know what I mean, right? The suspect tells the rehearsed story over and over again the same exact way. He memorized it and he's saying it like a speech, rather than something that he remembers.

In either case, I have nothing to hide. This is why I called her. I want her to help the police. I will do anything for anyone's help as long as I can get Harley back.

"Okay, get some rest now; we will be back in the morning," Leslie says, leaning over me and giving me a brief hug. Harold comes over and shakes my hand. I pull him in closer for a hug and he wraps his arms firmly around me.

"Thank you for calling us," he whispers into my ear, his voice cracking.

JACKSON

WHEN WE ALL SEARCH…

I spend the night tossing and turning. Whatever dreams I have are consumed by Harley. In one, she is walking down an aisle in a beautiful white dress about to marry me. In another, I use my hands to dig through black earth only to uncover her lifeless body. The dreams go back and forth between the world as it should be and the world as it could be, and I wake up from each covered in cold sweat. When I finally do fall asleep and my conscience lets me dream, a nurse with a group of trainees comes in to take my vitals and to ask me useless questions. They turn on the lights without even an apology and record their findings in my chart as well as in their computer. When they leave, they leave the lights on.

Frustrated and annoyed, I click the lights off using the remote on my bed and turn around to bury my face in the pillow. As I quickly start to drift off again, I suddenly realize that this is the first time since the accident that I actually turned my body without feeling excruciating pain. Either the drugs are working their magic or I'm recovering much faster than I thought I would.

Somehow, I manage to get a few good hours of uninterrupted sleep and when I finally open my eyes, the gloom of the morning is in full swing. The sun isn't shining and big droplets are hitting the window outside, but I feel refreshed and full of energy. My body still aches of course, but it feels nothing like it did yesterday.

And it's a good thing that I suddenly have this infusion of energy because half an hour later, my room is swarming with people. Aurora arrives first, carrying a green smoothie. Leslie and Harold come soon after. Leslie quickly starts to interrogate Aurora about everything that happened that night prior to Harley's kidnapping. She answers all the questions honestly except for one. Neither she nor I mention the fact that we almost kissed. No, correction. I don't mention that Aurora tried to kiss me and I pulled away and neither does she. That detail isn't relevant to the investigation and will only serve to hurt Leslie and Harold. They are Harley's parents after all.

Within the hour, two private investigators arrive. They come from the most highly recommended company in the city and they come prepared with the police report of the incident as well as a folder of paperwork and notes from their conversation with Detective Richardson.

"How did you get all that from the cops? I thought that they didn't reveal much to outsiders," Aurora asks Matthew Smith, the taller one with a more athletic build. His partner, Conner Stevens, is a bit older and heavier and with more suspicious eyes, replies, "We have a special relationship with the police department in the city."

"What Conner means by that is that we used to be cops. Detectives. I retired two years ago and Conner five. So we have a lot of connections."

"Friends," Aurora says.

"You could say that."

They ask me all the same questions that Leslie and the cops have asked before and I tell my story again. And again.

"I really wish that you would all share your notes," I say at the end. "I'm getting a little bit tired of saying the same thing over and over."

"We do share our notes," Matthew says.

"Sometimes going through it again lets you remember something you haven't before," Leslie adds.

I nod. I guess she's right. But I still don't see how this is going to help them find Harley.

"So...what is your plan?" I ask after Aurora goes through her version.

"What do you mean?" Matthew asks.

"What are you going to do to find her?"

The two private investigators exchange looks, as if I had asked the most insane question. I stare at them in disbelief.

"I mean, you do have a plan, right? What are you going to do about this?"

"We are going to the warehouse where they found the van and interview a few more people there."

"And what's that going to get you?"

"The next clue, hopefully."

That doesn't sound like enough. I didn't hire them to interview people. I hired them to find her.

"Didn't the cops do that already?"

"Maybe they missed something," Conner says.

"Or maybe they didn't, and you're just wasting your time."

Matthew shakes his head. "This is what we do, sir. Please let us do our jobs."

But panic is starting to rise within me. Anxiety is mixed with anger and rage.

"Your job is to find her. She's not at the warehouse. They switched cars. We all know this already!" My voice is elevated and frantic. I feel my heartbeat start to speed up. Blood rushes to my head and all I hear is its loud pounding between my temples.

"How do you propose we find her?" Conner asks, arrogantly. But that's the last thing I want to hear. If I could get out of this bed, then I'd punch him right in the face.

"I don't *fucking* know. It's not my job!"

The monitor next to me starts to beep out of control. My chest seizes up and two nurses run in and my vision goes black. When I open my eyes sometime later, I see only Aurora in the room with me. She's sitting curled up on the chair, asleep under her coat.

"Oh, hey! You're awake," she says, rubbing her eyes.

"Where is everyone?" I mumble.

"You got a bit too upset. The nurses kicked everyone out."

I nod. "What are they going to do to find her?" I whisper.

She walks over and takes my hand in hers. "It's going to be okay, Jackson.

"Leslie is going to go with them. She's going to make sure that they do their jobs."

I force a smile and lie back in bed. I want to believe her, but I don't. I should be the one looking for her. She is asking for me and I can't be there for her.

HARLEY

WHEN I TRY TO MAKE A FRIEND...

When Parker tells me that he wants me to sleep with him, my heart sinks. My hands clench up along with my jaw.

"C'mon, Harley. Didn't you hear me? You're sleeping with me."

He motions to the bedroom in which I changed into this ridiculous cheerleader outfit that he had wanted me to wear. Sam makes himself comfortable on the couch in front of the fire.

"Keep your fucking boots off the couch," Parker says. "Do you not have any class?"

Cowering his head like a small child, Sam does as he is told.

What is this power that Parker has over him?

Why does he do everything that he says? Why would he let him use his van and get involved with all of this in the first place?

Parker disappears into the bedroom, but I want to buy more time. I want to prolong my stay in the living room as long as possible.

"Was that your van that you used?" I ask. Sam looks up at me.

"Yeah, why?"

"Is it registered to you?"

He nods. I smile.

"Why?" He demands to know. "Why are you laughing?"

I shrug. "It's just funny."

"What is?"

"Parker got you to use your van for this. The cops are going to find it for sure. And then they'll trace it back to you."

"No, they won't." He shakes his head. But I can tell that my words have made an impact. He sits up a bit on the couch and looks up at me.

"Which part? That they'll find it or that they'll trace it back to you?"

He shakes his head. I've scared him enough. Now, I need to bring him in.

"Why are you doing this, Sam? What are you getting out of this?"

"Parker is my friend," he says, shaking his head.

I lower my voice to barely an audible whisper.

"Is that enough to spend your whole life in prison for? He's using you. He isn't looking out for you. You have nothing to do with this."

He looks at me as if he understands. Please, please, understand, I pray silently.

"You don't have to do this, Sam. You can just help me and I promise that I won't tell anyone."

"You won't tell anyone about what?" Parker comes out of the bedroom. Shivers run down my spine. Shit. Shit. Shit.

"Now, you aren't trying to fill my friend, Sam's, head with some of that old nonsense again, are you?"

I debate as to what I should do. Should I keep trying to get through to Sam or should I lie and pretend that I wasn't doing anything wrong?

"You think you can turn him against me?" Parker asks. "Still? You still think that?"

"I'm not trying to turn him against you."

"You're trying to get him to help you."

"I'm just trying to find out why he's helping you."

Parker leans on the door frame and crosses his arms in defiance.

"What if they find my van?" Sam asks. Just when I thought that all was lost, suddenly Sam is starting to have doubts. That's good. It's a seedling but it's also hope and that's all I need.

"What if they do?" Parker shrugs. "You're just parked in a warehouse, so what?"

"What if they know my license plate?"

"How could they?"

"That guy was chasing us. The one who got hit by a truck. He saw me pulling her into the van."

What? My blood runs cold. Someone saw us? Someone saw me get kidnapped.

"Who was that?" I ask.

"I don't know." Sam shakes his head. "He came out of that big house right where we picked you up."

Jackson. Jackson. Jackson!

My mind starts to race a mile a minute. The blackout took some of my memories and jumbled up the rest. But suddenly, it all becomes clear. It was Jackson who tried to help me. He yelled something right before Sam closed the door. And then he followed us?

"How do you know he followed us?" I ask.

"He saw him in the mirror. He was in a Bentley."

"Stop talking," Parker says.

"He probably saw my license plate number."

"I doubt that," Parker says confidently. But also a bit too confidently. Like he's trying to convince everyone about that fact, including himself.

"Besides, after I ran that red light and he followed me, he was hit by that truck. I doubt that he would've survived that. Not many people do."

Blood rushes to my head and suddenly I can't hear anything else. What is he talking about? What accident? Jackson was hit by a truck?

"Oh, you didn't know about that?" Parker laughs. He is enjoying this. "You didn't, did you?"

I see him laughing, but I don't hear him. My thoughts focus entirely on Jackson. He was hit by a truck trying to save me. And now...where is he now? I don't want to let myself go there, but I can't stop my stream of thoughts. I imagine his broken body being cut out of the car. The paramedics rushing him to the hospital. And then what? I don't know.

A part of me doesn't want to know. Here, he is my only hope. Not that I thought that he would come for me, but that he was there. Just alive and breathing and living his life. That was enough to keep me going. And now? Now, I don't know. I don't know what happens from here.

"C'mon, let's go," Parker says, grabbing my arm and pulling me out of my trance. No, I don't want to go. I resist, but he pinches my skin really hard and pushes me inside.

"Get on the bed," he hisses, closing the door behind us.

HARLEY

THAT NIGHT...

The room smells like stale cigarettes and body odor. The sheets are probably clean but the comforter is not. I can sense the dust rising off it.

But that's the least of my concerns. There's a strong bright overhead light shining in the middle of the ceiling that Parker asks me to turn off. Instead, he flips on the lamp on the nightstand, giving the room a softer more romantic glow. My breathing slows down to a stop. I know what he wants to do with me. Every girl knows. He's eying me in that way that creepy guys peer at us, not noticing the way that their faces contort in a mischievous ugly smile.

"Come here," he says, pointing to the bed.

It's the moment of truth. What do I do? Do I fight

him on this? Or do I just let it happen? I feel my body shutting down. A state of familiar shock is closing in around me. It makes it difficult to even move a muscle. I feel so helpless that all I really want is to close my eyes and pretend that this isn't happening.

"Come here," he says. I ignore him. Not so much in defiance but in my inability to move.

Parker walks up to me. His nostrils flare in anger and his eyes narrow with displeasure. I take a step back.

"Get away from me," I say, my back running into the dresser beside the door. Frantically, my hands search the top of it for something. What? Anything I can grab onto as a weapon. I finger a little dish, empty of knickknacks. It feels like it's made of porcelain. It's not very heavy or very big but it will have to do. The element of surprise is all I have.

He's standing right next to me. I can feel his sour breath on my face and it makes me want to vomit. He isn't touching me yet. Just eyeing me again. Looking at every part of me in admiration.

Then he brings his hands up to my face. He takes the ends of my hair and starts to twirl it in between his fingers.

"Come on, don't fight this. We can be so good together."

I swing my arm from behind my back and hit him as hard as I can with the dish. It stuns him and he takes a few steps back, disoriented. I don't let go of it and hit him again before he can utter a word.

"You bitch!" he yells, holding onto his bleeding nose. He grabs me by my shoulders and tosses me onto the bed. But I bounce onto my back and kick him as hard as I can before he can throw his body on top of mine. The move comes out of nowhere. I've never had any self-defense training, yet it seems to come from somewhere deep inside of me.

My kick sends him flying into the wall across from the bed and he hits his head on the flat television screen mounted there. As he writhes around in pain, I jump off the bed and run into the living room.

I run straight for the front door, but it's locked. When I reach for the dead bolt, Parker grabs me by my hair and pulls me away.

"Sam!" he yells at the top of his lungs. "Sam! Help me!"

We continue to struggle as he calls for Sam, who is nowhere to be found. I manage to kick Parker away from me again, but his grasp on my hair is stronger than I thought. The force of my kick pulls me closer to him. My head throbs from the pain but I keep fighting. Suddenly, Parker lets go. With my back to him, I run toward the door again. I unlock the top lock and reach for the handle. That's when the gun shot goes off, right next to my hand. The bullet misses me by millimeters, lodging a couple of splinters in my palm.

Startled, I turn around to face Parker's gun pressed to my forehead.

"If you make another move, I'm going to blow your head off."

My throat tightens and I can't inhale or exhale a breath. I freeze.

"Sam!" Parker yells. "Get the fuck out of the bathroom! Now!"

We wait in silence but no one appears.

"Don't make me come in there," Parker threatens. When no one comes out again, he backs up, making his way toward the small bathroom next to the fireplace.

"Don't move," he says, pointing the gun toward me. He kicks the door open only to discover that Sam isn't there. Then he walks over to the window, keeping the gun right on me, and peers into the darkness.

"Shit," he mumbles under his breath.

I don't need an explanation. Sam took off and that wasn't part of their plan.

He curses a few more times as he paces around the room, thinking. Finally, he grabs some duct tape from under the sink and tells me to turn around.

He wraps my hands behind my back as tight as he can. He looks around the room for something to tie me up to, eventually settling on the metal folding chair. He forces me into it and then wraps the tape around my chest. He also tapes my feet together at the ankles.

"Don't you fucking move an inch until I get back. If you do then I'll take that fire poker and shove it so far up your ass that you won't be able to walk again."

His words send shivers through my body and I sit perfectly still until I hear the car screech out of the driveway. Then, I don't waste a second.

I am not naive enough to know that he will ever let me go or ever let me get away with fighting him. No, this is my one and only chance. Without knowing it, Sam has given me an opportunity.

HARLEY

WHEN I TRY TO BREAK FREE...

When Parker was tying me up, I had pushed my body as far away from the chair as possible so that the tape wouldn't be that tight. I did the same thing with my wrists and ankles. They burned, but now I have an inch or so of wiggle room. I press as hard as I can against it to pull my feet apart, but it's not enough. The tape seems to only get stronger when I try to force it. The same thing happens when I try to pull my hands apart. I need a better plan.

I stand up with the chair on my back and hop over to the kitchen. There's a knife that Sam used to make himself a sandwich laying on the counter.

I can't reach for it with my hands so I sit back down into the chair and lift up my legs. I manage to kick it off the counter and onto the floor. I kick it to the middle of the room and then tilt to the side to fall onto the floor. The timing is crucial. If I don't get it just right then I will end up too far away from it and I don't know if I will be able to get up again from this position.

I take a deep breath and fall onto my right shoulder. The fall isn't without pain as my whole body and the metal chair fall onto one arm. But I don't let that faze me. I don't know how much time I have and I have to keep going.

I inch my way toward the knife. It takes me a few tries to get it in my left hand. I switch hands and tilt the blade upward and toward the tape. Then I start cutting.

The position of the blade is less than ideal and I have to take a few small breaks as my wrists start to cramp up. But I feel myself making progress. Finally, the tape starts to loosen. I slice a few more times and finally my hands break free.

"Yes," I whisper under my breath, too apprehensive to celebrate just yet.

Once my hands are free, I bring them around to the front and cut through the tape around my chest. This goes much faster and within another minute or so I get up from the floor.

"Oh my God," I say out loud. "I did it."

But this is just the beginning of the battle. When I open the door, a strong gust of wind hits me like a brick and I realize that I don't have any shoes. It's well below freezing and I won't get far in my bare feet.

I search the cabin frantically for a pair of shoes, but I don't find any. My mind is racing and I feel tears starting to well up in the back of my eyes.

"Stay calm. This isn't over," I say. "You just need to find an alternative."

I search the cabinets and the dresser. I find some old t-shirts that I consider wrapping around my feet. This will work a little bit, but there's snow on the ground and this won't be waterproof.

Under the kitchen sink, I find thick plastic bags.

"Okay, this will do."

I wrap my feet in three layers, careful to make sure that the part under my feet is as smooth as possible. Then I wrap them in two bags each, tying up them tightly around my ankles.

I take a few steps around the cabin to check their sturdiness. Once I'm satisfied with my construction, I put on the sweater I find in the closet over my cheerleader outfit. I also put on the large pants over my legs, tightening the belt as far as it will go. I roll up the pants so that they don't drag on the ground and trip me and put on the coat that I find in the main closet by the bathroom. Luckily, I also find a hat and a scarf. Once my winter outfit is ready to go, I run out of the door without another moment of hesitation.

In the driveway, I can see two lines in the snow where two vehicles were parked. I didn't notice the other one as it was parked beside the cabin and that must've been the car that Parker took to find Sam.

I run down the driveway, going fast but also pacing myself. I don't want to run too fast just yet in case I need to gun it later. At the end of the driveway, there are impressions in the snow that turn left, and I turn right to get as far away from them as possible.

The road is windy as it's carved in the middle of a hill. One side of it drops off and the other rises steeply above. I don't want to trot directly down the road in case the car that comes by is either Sam's or Parker's, but I also don't want to wander through the wilderness at night that's so close to the cabin. I need to get away from this place as fast as I can and I need to get to someone who will call the police for me.

The wind picks up and I press my coat tighter against my body to keep the cold out. My feet feel surprisingly comfortable in my makeshift shoes, but the wind is bone-chilling and I know that I need to find civilization soon.

At the bottom of the hill, the road straightens out and forms a two-lane highway. The road is straighter, but there's still a large hill going off the side of it. I don't know which way to turn so I again turn right. My trot turns into a fast walk as I get a cramp in my stomach. I'm not a big runner; in fact, I can't remember the last time I ever ran anywhere. I struggle for air but keep going anyway.

Peering into the darkness, I simultaneously pray for someone to drive by and for the road to remain empty. Someone driving by might be one of them and as long as I don't see another car, I'm safe. Yet, on the other hand, someone driving by might also be someone who could get me to safety faster than I can on my feet.

When my cramp disappears, I pick up the pace. Illuminated by nothing but the moon, I try to come up with a plan as to what to do next. If I see headlights, do I hide? Or do I try to flag them down? I won't be able to see much of the car so whatever I do will be a gamble.

The moment of truth arrives faster than I thought it would. Suddenly, a pair of headlights appears in the distance.

HARLEY

WHEN I HAVE TO MAKE A DECISION...

My heart jumps into my throat. What do I do? My mind starts to race, but my body makes the decision for me. I jump down the hill and hide. Even if the car does have a good person at the wheel, I can't risk running into Parker or Sam... I slide down the hill a bit and wait for the car to pass, holding my breath. Eventually, the sound of the engine roars past me and I let out a little sigh.

"Okay, it's going to be okay," I mumble under my breath to calm myself down.

When the coast feels clear, I pull myself up the side of the hill and peer down the road. And that's when I see them. The car's red taillights are a bit down the road away from me. They turn white as the driver backs up.

"Hey! Are you okay?" someone yells out through the rolled down passenger window. The voice doesn't sound anything like Parker's or Sam's and I let out a sigh of relief.

"Fine!" I yell. "I'm fine."

"I thought I saw someone jump down there, but I wasn't sure. I'm really glad that I decided to stop though," the man says. I climb up onto the road and look into the window. The man looking back at me is in his sixties with a smiling face and kind eyes.

"So...what are you doing here?" he asks.

I don't know what to say.

"Are you okay?"

I nod. "Do you think I can use your phone?"

"Um...sure, of course. Why don't you get in?"

I shake my head.

"I'd rather not," I say. "Please don't be offended, but I've been through something and I really just need to use your phone."

I decide it would be best to not trust him outright.

"There's nothing to be afraid of. Just let me know where you need to go and I'll take you there."

But I shake my head again. The more he insists on giving me a ride, the stronger that little voice in the back of my head says, no, no, no. This i good idea.

"Can I please just use your phone?" I ask again.

I look straight into his eyes and his demeanor changes. The smile vanishes and there's that familiar creepy look that appears on his face. Pursed lips mixed with a bit of desperation in his expression. Now, I know for sure that I can't trust him.

The creepy look vanishes just as quickly as it appears and the same forced smile comes back.

"Listen, why don't you just get in the car and warm up and then I'll let you use my phone," the man insists.

I've had enough. "No, thank you," I say and start to walk away from him. Driving backward, he pulls up to me again.

"Now, c'mon. Don't be like that, girlie. I'm just trying to be your friend."

That's it. Without another word, I turn toward the hill and start to make my way down. Luckily, the snow is thick here and the hill is relatively free of underbrush. Sliding my way down on my butt is surprisingly efficient. About halfway down, I get up and make my way through the thick snow.

"Where are you going?" I hear him scream down

at me from the road. "I was just trying to help you, you stupid bitch!"

I don't know exactly where that man was coming from, but I'm certain of one thing. His intentions were no good.

AT ANOTHER TIME, I probably would've second-guessed myself. I probably would've considered getting into his car just to not be rude. That's the kind of shit that goes through women's minds. But that man knew very well that he was threatening me. He didn't really want to help me; he just wanted me to get into his car. Well, no more.

As I make my way through the deep snow, I let out a big sigh of relief. One thing is for sure. That little voice in the back of my head, the one that makes the hairs at the nape of my neck stand up on end, that's the thing to listen to in times of potential danger. It's a sixth sense and you should always listen to it. It will never lead you astray.

The woods get deeper and deeper around me and with each step, I am getting further and further away from civilization. Only a short time ago, all I wanted was to run into another person and ask for help. But now? Now, the woods feel strangely comforting to me. At least, here, surrounded by nature, there isn't anyone around to hurt me. I may die of hypothermia, but that's a different kind of fear altogether.

When my feet get tired, I take a break by leaning on a tree, stripped of all of its leaves. It feels good to feel supported and I let my shoulders drop and relax for the first time since the kidnapping. As I slide down it, I realize that there's a tree trunk right under it. After clearing it of snow, I sit down and bury my head in my knees.

JACKSON

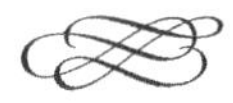

WHEN I GET SOME ANSWERS…

Dawn is just setting in, but I haven't slept in hours. I'm practicing walking. Everyone is telling me to take it easy, but my thoughts focus on only one thing. How I can regain my strength as fast as possible. Lying around and resting isn't going to work. There's only one way to do it. By actually doing it.

My legs feel weak after lying in the hospital bed, but they are getting stronger with each step. It's only now that I'm realizing how incredibly lucky I was to not only survive the accident, but to escape it with hardly any damage. External cuts and bruises don't really count.

Someone comes out carrying a tray of food that I had ordered. He remarks at how good I look given what happened. He knows who I am. Almost everyone whom I've come in contact with here seems to. I've seen the gossip magazines. I'm the recluse billionaire of Central Park who no one has seen in public in ages. According to some of the stories, I'm an eligible bachelor who is now paralyzed from the waist down. Those writers rarely get anything right.

After what feels like days without eating, I devour everything on the plate within minutes and place another order. I need fuel to build myself up again.

As I continue to pace around the room, from one corner to another, an old memory flashes into my mind. Lila was about fourteen months old and she was learning to walk. It took her about a month to gain the confidence to really walk around the house on her own. But once she did, there was nothing stopping her. I would sit in the living room watching television and she would just pace around the room for hours in awe of her own power. Occasionally, she would pause and reach for me, making a little pleading sound.

"Keep going, you can do it," I would say. Infused with newfound encouragement she would take one step and then another and another.

And so, here I am, all these years later doing the same thing. Tears start to well up in the back of my eyes, but I push them away. I can't think about Lila now. I can't mourn her because I need whatever strength I can summon to keep going. Lila is gone, but Harley might still be alive. And I need to find her.

Around seven o'clock, I finally decide to sit back down for a little bit of rest. I recline in the bed, put my feet up, and turn on the television. After mindless flipping through the channels, I turn it off again. The chatter and the bright lights give me a pounding headache.

Last night, my assistant showed up with my laptop and tablet and a new phone so I turn on the tablet for something soothing to watch on YouTube. I stumble on a video of tropical fish swimming around the corals and I lose myself in it for a while. One of the fish is bright yellow with little black and white lines and they swim in and out of corals, pecking at the top in search of food.

I've spent so much of my life working or hiding out in my house that it suddenly occurs to me that I've never been to the Caribbean. So many people I know own villas there, and yet, I've never even stepped my foot there. I watch a bright purple fish with scales that change color from lavender to mint as it glides along and I promise myself that that's where I'm going to take Harley when I find her. I want to sit next to her on a beach that's entirely ours. I want to snorkel with her in crystal blue waters and look at these fish in real life.

"Have you heard?" Aurora bursts into my room fueled by coffee and excitement.

I shake my head.

"They arrested one of the kidnappers!"

"Really? How?" My heart starts to beat frantically.

"The New Hampshire police arrested this guy in possession of a ton of crystal meth. He said that he wants to make a deal and told them that he knows about a girl who was kidnapped from New York City. Apparently they didn't believe him at first but after they checked the databases, they confirmed that he's talking about Harley."

"Oh my God," I whisper. "So, they found her?"

She checks her phone. After much debate, we had agreed that she would get the major updates from the private investigators just in case I needed to rest. I didn't so much agree to this but was forced into this situation by the doctors.

"No, they are working on the agreement right

now. He has to sign it before he will tell them where she is."

Suddenly, my jubilation at the news vanishes.

"What do you mean?"

"He's not telling them until they agree to the plea agreement is in place."

"But what if something happens to her in the meantime?"

She shakes her head. She doesn't have an answer to that because there is no answer.

When Detective Richardson comes by later that morning, her answers are no better than Aurora's.

"How long is this going to take?" I keep asking over and over. But she doesn't know. The real answer is that it's going to take as long as it takes and this guy, Sam Davis, knows that he has time on his side.

After taking a call, she comes back and tells me that it's finally over. Apparently, Sam got scared when the FBI told him that if they find her dead then the deal is off and he finally signed whatever agreement they came to.

My heart skips a beat at the thought. Dead. No, no, no. She's not dead. She's alive. We're going to find her alive, I say to myself.

"So, what's going to happen now?"

JACKSON

WHEN THEY'RE NOT ENOUGH...

Detective Richardson starts telling me about the details of the deal that Sam Davis got, as if I give a shit. For a moment, I stare at her dumbfounded, but then interrupt her to clarify my question.

"Where did he say she is?"

"They took her to some cabin they rented online in New Hampshire. They rented it the night before and the owner isn't there. It's all self-check-in apparently."

I inhale deeply trying to stay calm.

"So, this was planned?" Aurora asks.

Detective Richardson nods her head.

"Of course, it was planned. They had a van. They

watched her. They switched cars. They knew exactly where to take her," I say impatiently.

"So...why was this guy, Davis, out and about? Just scoring drugs?"

"Apparently, they had some sort of falling out. Him and Huntington," Detective Richardson explains. "He said that they had a fight and he took off, leaving Parker with Harley in the cabin. That's all he knows. When he got to town, he first got drunk in a bar and then bought a ton of crystal meth from an undercover cop."

I pace around the room, trying to figure out what to do. One thing is for sure. I can't just stay here and wait.

"Where is this cabin?"

"It's in a little town called Trader."

"But where exactly?" I ask.

"You want me to give you an address?" Detective Richardson takes a step back. "Why? What are you planning on doing?"

I shrug and shake my head. "Nothing. I just want to know."

"I've been doing this for a very long time, Jackson. You are not a loved one set on getting revenge for what happened."

"So, are you going to tell me or not?"

"No, absolutely not."

I shake my head.

"Listen, you need to just stay here and get better. They're going to take care of it. Everything is going to be fine."

I roll my eyes. "Do not make promises that you can't keep."

WHEN DETECTIVE RICHARDSON LEAVES, I go to the closet and get the clothes that my assistant brought over yesterday along with a phone and other tech devices. Aurora tries to stop me, but there's no way anyone can. I tell her that I feel better and that I'm going to New Hampshire. She wants to come along, but I say no. I need to take this long drive to clear my head and to figure out what I can do when I'm there. I also don't want to have her there second-guessing me.

Much to my dismay she brings the doctor and the nurse over to stop me. They insist that I need to stay for observation and that they are refusing to release me. I still don't care. I haven't committed a crime and I'm not a danger to myself. There's nothing they can do to keep me here.

"You have to sign your release paperwork." One of the nurses tries in vain as I walk out of the door.

"I offered to sign it already if you got it for me."

"It's not ready yet."

I shrug and continue walking down the hall. "Why don't you just bill me then?"

When I get out of the hospital, I hail a ride share on my phone and have him take me to my house. There I get straight into my BMW and head north.

The drive through the countryside is a lot more relaxing than I thought that it would be. I sit back in the seat, listen to some soothing music, and just space out. Not really space out, of course, but enough to relax and just let my hands and feet do what they are meant to do- drive without much of a thought.

A part of me thought that it may have been a good idea to bring Aurora or a driver for the drive just in case I had any flashbacks to the accident that nearly killed me. But luckily, I don't. In fact, I have no memory of it at all. All of my memories of that day focus on Harley, what happened to her, and the fact that I couldn't stop it.

When my thoughts drift there, I stop them and instead focus on what's ahead of me. What I know so far is that the kidnappers had a disagreement or a fight. But about what? It doesn't really matter, but it's a piece in the puzzle. Parker Huntington was behind this, but what about Davis? Did he trick him into it somehow? Or did he go along with it until a certain point and then decided that it was too much?

Given how obsessed Parker has been with Harley, I doubted that he would be willing to share her. That thought sends shivers through my body, but it's something that I have to consider. And if he wasn't willing to share her, then what? Did Davis get upset and storm out, leaving Harley at Parker's mercy?

I grasp onto the steering wheel so hard that my knuckles turn white. I have to get to Trader, New Hampshire, as fast as possible. She's there and she needs me. I didn't save her once, but I will do it this time.

As human beings we all make promises that we can't keep. I don't know why exactly except that they are promises that we want to keep. Perhaps there's something about the process of promising that gives us hope. I don't know if this is a promise that I can keep, but I make it anyway. It's the only thing that I can do.

When my phone's GPS says that I have arrived in Trader, New Hampshire, I pull over to a diner. I've had hours to think about how to find her without knowing the exact location of the cabin. And I did come up with one plan.

When I was a kid, I loved listening to police scanners. I loved knowing what was going on and where the action was. On my way here I realized that there is a chance that whatever was going on at the cabin would be announced on the police scanner. The FBI and the local police are probably setting up a perimeter around the cabin and dispatching officers there. I don't know whether my reasoning is sound, but it's the only idea that I had come up with.

Of course, I don't have a police scanner on me and that's where the internet comes in. I could probably buy one at the local Walmart, but I open my laptop, set up a hotspot, and decide to first check for a broadcast online.

I type in police scanner and Trader, New Hampshire, into the search bar and click on the top result.

Aha! There it is! The voices come in loud and clear.

I pull out of the parking lot and drive up one of the winding streets listening to the chatter. Nothing so far, but I'm not giving up hope that easily.

JACKSON

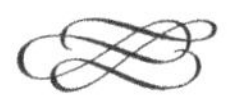

WHEN SNOW STARTS TO FALL...

I drive around the town in circles, listening to the police scanner but hear nothing significant. Snow is starting to fall and the roads get covered in a thin layer of flakes. It's not thick or deep enough yet to be dangerous or difficult to drive through so for now I just enjoy the view. After about an hour, I try to figure out what to do next. There's a good possibility that whatever happened at the cabin is already over and I arrived too late. Maybe they even rescued her already. But then I would probably get a phone call, right?

I have no idea. I would assume so, but I did leave under pretty bad circumstances. Maybe they're still holding a grudge.

Suddenly, the music comes to a stop and a phone call appears on my dashboard. It's Leslie Burke, Harley's mother. In my rush to get out of New York, I had completely forgotten about her.

"Where the hell are you?" Leslie asks. There's no hello or how are you.

"New Hampshire. In a town called Trader."

"Why are you there?"

"Because that's where the cabin is. That's where they took her."

She pauses for a moment.

"Look, I'm sorry I didn't tell you. It actually completely slipped my mind. But I should have."

Still angry, she takes a deep breath and asks, "Do you know where this cabin is?"

"No, Richardson didn't tell me. She didn't exactly want me to go."

"It wasn't the best idea."

I shrug and forget that she can't see me.

"So, what are you doing there?"

"Driving around, listening to the police scanner."

"Hmm...good idea. You get anything?"

"Nope. You think there's any chance they aren't broadcasting this?" I ask.

"Not sure."

Neither of us say anything for a moment.

"I should be there, you know," Leslie finally says. "I was instrumental in making that deal with Davis. In getting them to hurry the fuck up."

She's right. I fucked up. "I'm sorry. I was really not thinking."

After telling me to be in touch if I hear anything, she hangs up.

I feel like a total ass. How could I forget about her? When this first happened, I was so desperate to get anything to help that I reached out to Harold and to the private investigators just to get more answers. But as soon as I was able to move again and had my strength back, I had completely put them out of my mind.

I thought that I could do this by myself. I thought that just getting here was enough. How big could this town be anyway? It wasn't like it was New York. But the reality is that I don't know anything. I don't know the first thing about finding her. And now that my plan to listen to the police scanner and hear the location of the cabin and to just show up here doesn't work, then what? How do I actually find her?

I pull over by the side of the road and pick up my phone and text Aurora.

Have you heard anything? What's going on?

I know that she's angry with me and probably

doesn't want to talk, but I hope that she will still tell me something about what's going on if she knows anything.

Then I dial Detective Richardson's number. On the third ring she finally answers.

"What do you want?" she asks with a disapproving tone.

"I'm here. In Trader."

"So what? Do you want a medal or something?"

"No, I want to know if you know anything. Like the location of the cabin?"

She lets out a big sigh. "I don't want you there. You shouldn't have gone up there."

"I know. I know. But I'm here now...is there anything you can tell me?"

"No," she says a bit too fast. I get the feeling that she's lying.

"Please, you have to tell me. I'm here. I want to see her. I want to help her."

"You can't help her. The FBI are there. The local police. The state police. What the hell are you going to do but interfere with the investigation?"

This makes me angry. My nostrils flare as blood rushes to my head and pounds in between my temples.

"This isn't just a *fucking* investigation to me. She's

my girlfriend. No, more than that. She's the love of my life. I don't care about the investigation as long as I can get her back."

The words come out like an avalanche out of me. All at once.

"That's the whole problem," Detective Richardson says quietly. "That's exactly why you can't be up there. That's exactly why you can't be a part of this."

Before I can say another word, she hangs up. I stare at the screen on my dashboard for a few moments before pounding my hands on the steering wheel. I grab onto the wheel and shake it, thrashing against it. I try to force it to absorb my anger, but it simply bounces it back to me.

The inside of the car starts to feel like it's closing in on me. With claustrophobia setting in, I put the car in park and get out. Out in the fresh air, I let out a loud yelp and all of my anger and hate suddenly has somewhere to go. I open my hands out wide and stretch toward the sky. I've never been a religious person, but now I am asking for help from anyone who might be listening. From God and the spirit world and nature.

"Please, please, help me find her," I whisper under my breath.

Thick, wet snowflakes fall on my face. I can't help but stick out my tongue and enjoy them melting in my mouth. Two blackbirds fly from one tree to another across the highway and somewhere in the distance a car engine echoes through the hills.

JACKSON

WHEN I FIND SOMETHING OUT...

I take a few long deep breaths, holding the icy cold air in my lungs for as long as possible before exhaling. Finally, I start to feel calm enough to get back into the car. The anger and frustration and rage are still there, but instead of being right at the surface, they seem to have recessed somewhere deeper.

I get back in the car but leave the driver's door ajar. I glance at my phone. Aurora read my message but hasn't replied to it. I dial Matthew Smith's number. He has heard through the grapevine that I've left the hospital and came up here and he's not happy about it just like Richardson. But unlike her, he's my employee with an hourly contract.

"You really shouldn't have gone up there—" he starts to say, but I quickly interrupt him.

"I know. But I had to."

"I would've come with you."

I now realize that it would've been smarter for me to invite the private investigators whom I've hired. They are retired cops and experienced in finding people. But frankly, that didn't occur to me at the time.

"I thought that you were going to try to stop me like Aurora and Richardson. And I just...needed to get here as soon as possible."

I get the sense that he knows that I didn't call to talk about my mistakes.

"I actually have some news."

"Really?" I ask with a mixture of excitement and fear.

"I don't know if I should be telling you this—"

"Tell me."

"I should really be there with you—"

"Tell me," I interrupt him again.

"I found the address of the cabin."

I start the engine without a second thought.

"What is it?"

"You promise you won't do anything stupid?" he asks. "If you interfere with this investigation and something goes wrong, the FBI and the police are going to blame me. You know that."

"Yes, yes, I won't," I promise. I'm not listening to any of his words. At this point, I would promise to do anything to get the information that I want.

Finally, he tells me the address.

I put it into the GPS on my phone and take off. It's only 1.7 miles away from me.

Matthew wants to stay on the line to hear what happens. I give him this courtesy.

"How did you find out where it is?" I ask as I drive along the winding road.

Snow is falling at a faster rate now. The little snowflakes that peppered the roads before are now creating almost whiteout conditions.

"I have a lot of sources. I know a lot of people, some of them like to talk."

"Uh-huh." I nod, barely hearing him over the pounding of my heart.

"That's why you hired me, right?" he asks, rhetorically. "Because I'm good at my job?"

"Yeah, I guess," I say, absentmindedly.

My hands are ice cold and wrapped tightly around the steering wheel. I don't care about the speed limit. The only thing slowing me down is the curves in the road.

"Listen, you have to stay calm," Matthew says as I drive up a large hill. I'm less than a tenth of a mile away now.

"No matter what happens, you have to stay calm."

"Okay."

"Promise me."

"I promise," I say, but I don't even know what I just promised.

Finally, I'm here.

I see the cabin in the distance surrounded by police vehicles and paramedics. Bright yellow police tape goes all around the perimeter. People holding professional cameras pointed at people with microphones are standing just outside the taped off portion.

I put the car in park and run outside without bothering to close my door.

"What's going on here?" I walk up to a random bystander.

"They were supposed to find that girl who got kidnapped here."

"Did they?"

"Nope," the man says.

"What do you mean?"

He shrugs and points me toward one of the media people who he's trying to listen to.

I walk up to one of the police officers guarding the perimeter.

"Did you find anyone inside? What's going on?"

"Please stand back, sir."

"You have to tell me. I know her. She's my girlfriend," I plead.

His demeanor softens for a moment, but then the same coldness returns.

"I really can't tell you anything."

"Why are the paramedics here?" I ask.

"Please stand back."

I shake my head and lift up the tape. But I only make a few steps toward the cabin when he and another cop physically grab me.

"You can't be here!" one of them yells into my ear. They pull me back to the other side of the tape.

"If you do that again, you're going to get arrested," he says, still holding onto my arm.

"Is she there? Can you tell me that?"

"No, she's not. There's no one there," the other cop hisses. "We are processing the place as a crime scene so if you want to find her, you better stay the fuck out."

The words come out with so much force that a drop of his saliva lands on my cheek.

"Okay, thank you. I promise I won't," I say, and finally they let me go. "What about Parker? Parker Huntington? Did you find him?"

"What do you know about him?"

"He's the one who kidnapped her. He has been stalking her for a while. Do you know where he is?"

"Maybe," one of the cops says with a blank expression. "Maybe not. Don't cross this line again."

I stay put. Placing my hands in my pockets, I remember that I placed my phone there. I pick it up and bring it to my ear. Matthew is still there.

"Did you hear all that?" I ask.

"They don't know shit."

"Yeah, or they aren't saying shit," I say.

I walk over to one of the news people and listen in on their broadcast.

"Unfortunately, neither the suspect, Parker Huntington, or the victim of the kidnapping, Harley Burke, are anywhere to be found."

My heart sinks. This is what I've been afraid of the whole time. He took her somewhere else.

HARLEY

WHEN SNOW STARTS TO FALL...

With the cold setting in, my body is suddenly starting to feel warm. The pain at the tips of my fingers, which felt like a thousand different tiny needles pricking at me all at once dissipates. At first, I feel like the weather is getting warmer, but looking around I know that this is not the case. A strong gust of wind blows past the tree at the same strength as it did when I was cold. No, this is something else altogether. It's not that I'm getting warmer; it's that hypothermia is setting in.

It takes all of my strength to struggle back up to my feet and pull myself away from the tree.

"You have to keep going," I say over and over. "If you don't then you'll freeze to death."

After I take a few steps, blood starts to circulate through them again, sending a shooting pain up my legs.

"Pain is good," I whisper. "Pain means that I can still feel my toes."

As I walk further and further into the woods, I debate the possibility of going back to the road. The creepy driver is undoubtedly gone by now, but still something keeps me from there. It's too close to the cabin.

Parker is probably back by now and has already discovered that I am gone. That means that he will be searching for me, unwilling to let me get away that easily. And that road is too close and too straight. If I run into his car, he will not let me get away that easily. And I am too weak now to fight him off.

Hours pass as I continue to stumble through the snow. I do not make the mistake of sitting down and taking a rest again out of fear of not being able to get up. No matter how much my body screams for a little reprieve, I don't give in. Finally, the sun appears over the horizon and morning is here. Light gives me new hope even though I do not know how far I am from civilization, let alone safety.

Sometime later, I finally see it. A little street with three small houses and cars out front. The cars are old and two of them are trucks. What should I do now? I wonder. I could come right up and knock and ask for help, but who will I find on the other side? Men are more likely to drive trucks and another man is not someone that I want to see right now.

So, I decide to wait. For what? I'm not sure except that I need a sign that I will be safe. I walk in circles to keep myself warm, but now my feet are starting to ache for another reason altogether. The t-shirts wrapped around them as makeshift shoes have rubbed against my feet all night, etching away at my skin and leaving behind sores.

Just as I'm about to sit down and try to tighten and adjust the wraps, I see her.

A woman in a light blue puffy jacket and a white slouchy hat comes out with her child who is about five years old. They walk to the street and check the mailbox. The child starts to play in the snow as the woman looks through the envelopes.

This is my chance.

I take a deep breath and start to walk towards her, waving.

"Hi...I'm sorry to bother you but...can you help

me?" I ask. My voice is shaky and uneven. When she turns to face me, she first looks me up and down before asking me what happened.

"I was attacked and kidnapped and he took my shoes. I've been wandering around all night and..." I can't keep talking. I cough to clear my throat and then ask to use her phone.

"Why don't you come in and warm up first?"

"I don't want to impose..."

"Nonsense. Please come in."

It's hard to put into words how grateful I feel at this moment. After everything I've been through, I don't want to impose on her. I'm a stranger after all, and I don't want to make her feel uncomfortable bringing an unknown person into her home. But her invitation and insistence on taking in me overwhelms me with emotion.

"It's going to be okay," she whispers in my ear as I burst into tears.

MARIE BRINGS me a cup of tea and puts on cartoons for her son. Her house is small but incredibly cozy and comforting. The tea warms me up immediately and I even remove the crocheted throw that she wrapped around me.

"I think it's time to pull off your shoes," she says, kneeling down next to me.

"Oh, no, I can do it myself."

"Nonsense, let me help you. I'm a medical professional."

Marie is about forty years old and is a nurse practitioner. Her hands are sturdy and confident and her whole demeanor puts me at ease.

"I really hope that you didn't get frostbite out there."

"Me, too."

I watch as she pulls off the plastic bags from my feet and then unwraps the t-shirts.

"They don't look too bad," she says with a sigh of relief. "You have a lot of abrasions, of course, but no frostbite."

She applies some ointment and puts on some adhesive bandages to cover up the sores. Then she hands me a pair of fluffy socks that feel like heaven.

"Thank you so much for...everything."

The words express gratitude but they hardly scratch the surface of explaining how thankful I am for her help.

After her son goes to his room, she asks me more

about what happened. Feeling safe, I decide not to hold back and tell her about everything in detail. She listens carefully, shaking her head in disbelief. When I'm done, she turns to me and asks, "Do you want to call the police?"

HARLEY

WHEN I HAVE TO MAKE A DECISION...

Do I want to call the police? It's such a simple question and yet for some reason I can't answer it. Prior to getting to Marie's house, it was all I wanted. Just the opportunity to call the authorities. But now? Now, going through the story and everything that I've been through with a bunch of strangers feels too daunting of a task. I told Marie because she was kind and comforting and loving to me. But the police? You never know what kind of cop you're going to get. Some are judgmental. Others are just cold.

"You have to call them, you know that, right?" Marie asks. "I looked you up on my phone. Everyone's looking for you."

"They are?"

"Yes." She hands me her phone and shows me the string of search results.

I take another deep breath.

"What's holding you back?" she asks.

"I just don't want to go into all that right now. I mean, I'm so tired and I just need to get some sleep. But I don't want to be a bother to you anymore."

She nods.

"You can stay here for as long as you want."

I smile. "Thank you, but I have imposed on you too much as it is."

"So, what are you going to do? The town is about five miles away. You can't walk there. Do you want a ride there?"

"No...I don't want to go to town."

The thought of running into Sam or Parker by accident scares me to my very core.

"Is there anyone else you can call?" Marie asks.

"Yes, there is!"

There's only one number that I know by heart. I dial it and wait. It takes a few rings for Julie to answer.

"Hello?" she asks, her voice is tentative and unsure.

"Julie? It's Harley."

There's a long pause.

"Oh my God! Harley! Where are you? Everyone's looking for you."

"I'm fine. I got away and I'm safe now."

"Are you with the police?"

"No…I haven't called them yet."

There's another long pause.

"Why the hell not?"

"I couldn't…I wanted to call you first," I say. It's difficult to explain, but I take a deep breath and jump right in. "I need to know something."

"What?"

"Jackson? Is he…dead?"

I tried not to think about this possibility the whole night because if I thought about it too much then I wouldn't have had the strength to keep going. But now, the moment it takes her to respond feels like a decade.

"You don't know?"

"I know he was hit by a truck. But that's it. Please, tell me the truth. Whatever it is."

I hold my breath. Another decade passes.

"Harley, he's fine. He got out of the hospital soon after he woke up and he's there looking for you."

It takes me a moment to process this information.

"What do you mean, here?"

"You're in New Hampshire, right? Well, he found out where the cabin is that they took you to and he drove straight up. He's still there in Trader."

"Hold on a sec." I pull the phone away from my head and turn to Marie.

"Where are we right now? Exactly?"

"Trader, New Hampshire," she says without missing a beat.

My head starts to spin. Jackson is here, looking for me. He's fine. He's alive and searching. I sit back down on the couch because I fear that my legs are about to give out.

"Can you tell me his number? I don't have my phone."

I DIAL the number as soon as I hang up with Julie. I don't waste a moment. My hand shakes as I bring the phone to my face and wait. He answers it on the first ring.

"Jackson?" I whisper. My voice cracks, so I clear my throat and repeat his name.

"Harley? Harley? Where are you? Are you okay?" he rattles off.

"I'm fine. Everything's fine. I got away from them."

"Where are you?"

I put him on speaker phone so that Marie can tell him her address.

"Julie said that you are here in Trader."

"I'll be there in three minutes."

My heart jumps into my throat. Oh my God. He's actually coming. I'm going to see him again. And wrap my arms around him and kiss him.

"Harley? Are you there?"

I nod and try to answer but nothing comes out except for tears.

"She's fine," Marie says. "She's just overwhelmed."

"Thank you so much for helping her," he tells her.

"Of course."

A few minutes later, a car pulls up to the front of the house and Marie opens the door. Jackson takes me into his arms and lifts me up off the floor. He spins me around and presses his lips onto mine.

"You're fine. You're fine. You're fine," he says into my ear over and over again. It's almost as if he's trying to convince himself that this is really happening.

Tears flow down my face and my throat closes up with each sob. After he puts me down, he wipes my tears and kisses my hands. Marie invites us inside. I limp as I take a few steps, so Jackson lifts me up and carries me to the couch.

"What have they done to you?" he whispers under his breath. I can sense the anger in his tone.

"Parker took my shoes, but I managed to break free and make some makeshift shoes out of some clothes and plastic bags."

"And you wandered around all night in them?"

I nod.

"I'm so, so sorry," he says, wrapping his arms around me. "I should've come out sooner, but I had no idea you had come to see me. All I heard was the gunshot and then I saw someone pushing you into the van and then you were gone."

My mind goes back to that moment. And then it rewinds a little further. I'm standing on his stoop watching a woman touching his face, reaching for him. Throughout all this, I had managed to put that memory out of my mind as well. That is until now.

HARLEY

WHEN WE TALK...

Marie gives us some space by taking her son on a walk and leaving us alone in her house. Jackson sits next to me on the couch and takes my hand in his. There's a big wide smile painted on his face.

"I can't make it stop," he says, laughing and pointing to his lips.

"I don't want you to," I say, kissing the back of his hand. He puts his hand on the back of my neck and pulls me closer to him. When our lips touch, I pull away.

"What's wrong?"

I shake my head. I don't really want to talk about it now. I want to enjoy the moment. I want to be with him without thinking about the complications. I don't want to be mad at him. I don't want to wonder if he is lying to me. I just want things to be the way they were back then, before all of this happened.

"No, I'm sorry," Jackson says right away. "Of course. You've been through so much. I don't want to pressure you in any way."

I shake my head again.

"Can I just hold your hand?" he asks. I nod. His palms are soft and smooth, but strong at the same time. I like how small my hands feel wrapped inside of his. We sit here in silence for a few moments. He is giving me space and I appreciate it. But with each minute that passes, this thing that's separating us seems to take up more and more room.

"I didn't want to bring this up before, but now I can't really stop thinking about it," I finally start.

"What is it?"

"I got all of your letters and I really appreciated them."

"I'm glad."

"I went to your house that night because I wanted to talk to you. But I didn't come in because I looked through the window and saw...her."

Jackson narrows his eyes.

"There was a woman with you. I saw her run her fingers through your hair and just...touch you."

I wait for him to deny it. I wait for him to lie to cover up the truth. But the expression on his face suddenly changes; it's as if a light bulb goes off.

"Oh, that's Aurora. My ex-wife."

"Why was she there?"

"Her husband beat her up pretty good, gave her a black eye and everything. She's thinking of separating from him and she was in New York so she came to see me."

As he speaks, he looks me straight in the eye. His words are frank. His honesty is obvious. He is either the best liar in the world or he is telling the truth.

"Oh," I mumble.

"She helped me buy the house and we have been staying in touch recently. So, that's why she's staying with me."

Staying with him? The words ring in my ears creating an echo. I didn't know that. I don't know what I thought before, basically that she was just some girl. But now...

"You have nothing to worry about," he says, lifting my chin up to his face. "I love you."

I nod and look away from him.

"You don't believe me?"

I shrug. "No, I do. I just...I thought that what I

saw back there through the window was more than just...friendship."

I don't know how else to put it, but he has to know. He doesn't respond for a moment and I hold my breath, hoping that he does not deny my feelings. I've met men who have told me, no you shouldn't feel this or that and that's one of the hardest things to hear. It's the same thing as saying, 'your feelings don't matter. What you feel is insignificant.'

"You're right," Jackson says after a moment.

"About what?"

"What you saw back there wasn't just friendship."

My heart sinks. At once, I am both relieved and terrified by this statement.

"Maybe I shouldn't tell you this, but I don't want to lie. I will never lie to you."

I feel all the blood drain away from my face.

"What happened?" I whisper quietly.

"We have a long history together. Aurora and I. And a complicated one. There was a time when I thought that we were in love. We even started a family together. But then one day, she just took off. She left Lila when she was just a baby and she never came back. She married some asshole who is a prince of Luxembourg and he has always treated her like shit and she preferred his company to her daughter's."

I nod.

"The anger that you hear in my voice has nothing to do with my feelings for her. It just pisses me off that my daughter never got to have a mother, because outside of some of her issues, she is a wonderful person and Lila would've loved her very much."

"I'm really sorry," I say, taking his hand in mine.

"It doesn't matter now, she's gone, right?" he says, shrugging his shoulder, and all I can see is the pain coursing through his body.

I wait for him to continue. That moment that I saw seems so insignificant to all of this and yet it's all I can think about.

"Aurora has always had issues with me. I treated her right, but that was a turn off for her. It's like she needs to have toxicity in her life just to feel alive," Jackson says after a moment. "Before you saw what you saw...I had just walked in on her making out with Elliot Woodward, remember him?"

Shivers run down my spine. He's another asshole who thinks that he's entitled to whatever the hell he wants.

"Anyway, we were talking about that and I was telling her that there are good men in the world and she deserves to be with someone who will treat her right." His voice trails off for a moment. "And then she leaned over and tried to kiss me."

HARLEY

WHEN WE GET BACK...

Jackson stops talking and I stare at him, waiting for him to continue.

"Aurora tried to kiss me but I pushed her away," Jackson says. "I'm not sure what part of that you saw, but that's what happened."

I nod and look down at the floor.

"I don't want her, Harley. I don't want anyone else, but *you*."

My mouth forms into an unwilling smile.

"Do you believe me?" he asks. I shrug. I pretend that I don't believe him, but deep down I know that he's telling me the truth. He didn't have to tell me any of this. He could've denied it entirely, but he didn't.

"Do you believe me?" Jackson asks again.

I nod.

"Tell me out loud. I need to hear it."

"I believe you," I say after a moment. I reach over and pull him close to me. When our lips touch, everything feels okay again. In this kiss, it's as if nothing has happened. We never had a fight. We never pulled apart. They never took me. Everything that has occurred suddenly vanishes.

He pulls me closer to him and I lose myself in his mouth. His hands bury themselves in my hair and I run my fingers up and down his chest. When I pull away from him and stare into his eyes the world is back to the way it's supposed to be.

"I love you," he says.

"I love you, too."

He kisses me again.

"Thank you for looking for me," I mumble through our pressed lips. "That means...so much."

"I'm just sorry that I couldn't help you sooner."

"I can't believe that you were hit by a truck. That must've been so..."

"I was really lucky. Very few people survive something like that, let alone with no injuries."

I run my fingers over the large bandage on the right side of his forehead. There are other scratches and bruises all over his face as well.

“What about all these?” I ask.

“These don’t count,” he whispers in my ear and pulls my mouth toward his again.

Somewhere behind us the door opens and Marie and Thomas come in.

“I hope I’m not interrupting anything,” she says with a little mischievous smile.

“No, no, of course not. Let me help you with that.” Jackson jumps up and takes the bags that she’s carrying away from her.

“Wow, a gentleman. That’s a keeper.”

WHILE JACKSON HELPS Marie prepare a few sandwiches for lunch, I decide to take a nap. With my adrenal system running on full blast this whole time, I suddenly find it impossible to fight my body shutting down much longer. Marie shows me to her bedroom and I fall asleep as soon as my body hits her comforter.

It’s dark when I wake up and stumble back into the living room. Jackson is playing a board game with Thomas while Marie is crocheting. They immediately jump to help me and offer me something to eat. After filling my belly with some homemade bread, I'm ready to talk.

"I think we should call the police," Jackson says. I've been expecting this and I'm sure that Marie has told him about my trepidation about this already.

"I'm sure that you don't want to, I wouldn't want to either. But people are looking for you. And they deserve to know."

I nod.

"Is that a yes?" he asks. I nod again and take another big bite of the sandwich.

THE NEXT TWENTY-FOUR hours are a blur. I talk to cops and the FBI in New Hampshire. I tell them the same story over and over again and then we drive down to New York and I tell more cops the same story. Sam Davis is under arrest and he cooperated with them to get leniency on the crystal meth possession charges.

"We all thought that you were being held at the cabin and he gave us the location of the place," Detective Richardson explains as if I'm an idiot.

"And what did you give him in exchange for that information? I mean, in terms of my kidnapping."

The eager expression on her face falls and is replaced by something that resembles defensiveness.

"We didn't have another choice, Harley."

I shake my head. I know what she's going to say before she says it.

I glance at Jackson who is sitting next to me in the precinct's interview room. He averts his eyes.

"Did you know about this?" I ask.

"We were out of options, Harley. He was our only lead." I ignore him.

"So, what deal did he get? I didn't hear you," I ask Detective Richardson.

"The prosecutor dropped all charges in connection with this case."

I get up so fast from my chair that it actually knocks backward and tips over. Jackson reaches for it as I start to pace around the room.

"So, he's free? Sam Davis, the asshole who pushed me into that van, the guy who Parker couldn't have done this without...he's just going to be walking around the city...free as a bird? Is that right?"

Detective Richardson looks away from me.

"And what about Parker? Where is he?"

"We don't know. We're looking for him."

"Any deals you want to make with him in exchange for some information?" I ask sarcastically.

"I don't deserve to be treated like this, Harley. I know that you're angry. But we did the best we could."

I shake my head in anger. I try to take myself back to that peaceful moment at Marie's house, but I simply can't. Talking to all of these law enforcement officers over these last twenty-four hours has fueled the fire around everything about how my case has been handled.

"The thing that really pisses me off is that you didn't even need to find that fucking cabin. Sam took off because he was scared and Parker took off after him. I broke out of my restraints and I was the one that freed myself. I was the one who ran away from that other creep who wanted me to get into his car. I was the one who hiked all night until I found a safe place to reach out to you from. You all...didn't do shit."

JACKSON

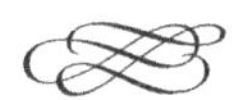

WHEN I TRY TO MAKE PEACE...

I don't know what to say or do to make things better. At the time, I would have done anything to save her. I didn't think we had much time and I wanted to get to the place where they were holding her as soon as possible. Just in case something worse had happened. But how was I supposed to know that she didn't need our help? Or rather that by the time we learned about the cabin, she had already escaped.

There is no way to know, that's how. We all work with imperfect information at all times. If we knew everything then there would be nothing to learn from anything. Still, I can't shake the feeling of regret. It seems to permeate throughout my whole body, filling every nook and crevice.

"I know that you are upset-" I start to say.

"I'm more than upset. I'm mad as hell," Harley says as we walk out of the precinct.

"I wanted to get to you as soon as possible. We all did."

"And if you'd found me dead or raped, then what? Would he walk on those charges, too?"

"I'm not sure about rape, but no, I don't think he would get immunity if you weren't found alive."

She paces in circles around me.

"I just don't know how to deal with this. I mean, I thought that I could get some justice. But now, Sam is out free, walking around as if he didn't do anything. And Parker? He's still a threat. No one knows where he is and I doubt that they'll find out."

"Why?" I ask.

"He's getting smart. A lot smarter than he was before. More devious, too. When he first started stalking me, it felt like he was harmless. Like he just had this little crush on me. But over these years with each thing escalating and getting worse…it just feels like one day…he's going to kill me."

She turns toward me and I see tears running down her cheeks. She buries her face in my shoulder and I wrap my arms tightly around her.

"That's not going to happen, sweetie. I will do everything in my power to stop that."

After sobbing a few times, she pulls away.

"That's the thing though," she says. "It's not in your power. He could be watching us right now for all you know. No one can do anything about it."

I shake my head in defiance.

She can't be right. No, she's wrong. I can protect her. But how?

"Can you take me home?" she finally asks. I nod. As we pull out of the parking lot, I ask her. I realize that I'm not entirely sure what she means by home.

"Do you want me to take you to your place or mine?"

She laughs.

"Oh, I'm sorry, yeah, I wasn't clear, was I?" Harley asks, laughing. This is the first smile I've seen since I first saw her at Marie's and it makes my heart feel good to see it again.

"Actually, I was referring to your place. If you don't mind, of course."

I smile and put my hand on her knee. "No, of course not."

WHILE I DRIVE SLOWLY through the congested Manhattan streets, I try to think of some way that I can protect Harley from Parker. The first thing to do is to take her away from the places that he knows she goes to. He knows where she lives so she shouldn't go back there. He knows where I live so my home is also not very safe. It's bigger, of course, with a lot more security, but out on the street, she is not safe.

What else does Parker know? Or rather, what else can Parker find out?

"I think maybe we should hire security," I say. "Just to have some protection before we can figure more things out."

"Yeah, maybe," she says absentmindedly.

"There's a reason why people get bodyguards. They're good at their jobs. They keep people safe."

"I can't live my life like that though. Cooped up, away from society."

I glance at her, skeptically.

"What?"

"Okay, don't take this the wrong way, but it's not like you did all that much stuff before I met you. You're kind of a homebody," I say.

She smiles.

"Homebodies are pretty easy to keep safe."

She shakes her head and rolls her eyes at my attempt at humor.

"What do you mean by before we can figure more things out?"

"Like a more permanent solution to keeping you safe. Before they find him, that is."

"You keep saying that, but what do you mean by that?" She challenges me.

"I was thinking that maybe we should take a break from New York. Get away to some place where he can't find us."

She nods her head. I get the sense that she thinks this is a good idea.

"But your life is here. Your business is here. I wouldn't want to impose—" she starts to say but I cut her off.

"I've run my business from inside my home for nearly four years. I can do it from just about anywhere else in the world as well."

When we pull into my garage, she is smiling. We don't have a plan yet, but we're close to it. I let out a big sigh of relief. All I want to do now is to take her upstairs and kiss her over and over again.

As we enter the house, her arms are draped over my neck and my hands are planted firmly on her hips. In the foyer, we stand for a moment in the dark and I let my mouth find her.

Suddenly, a flash of bright lights interrupts our reverie.

Harley pulls away from me and says, "Mom?"

JACKSON

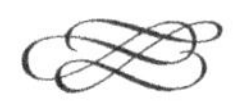

WHEN WE REST...

Leslie Burke stands next to Harold, holding his hand. She is leaning on him for support, not just physically but also emotionally. When Harley sees her, she is so caught off guard that she takes a step back and lands on my foot.

"Mom? What are you doing here?"

Her father, who looks like he has aged three years during this ordeal, wraps his arms around her and pulls her close to him. Harley quickly reciprocates and they stand there in their embrace for a while. When they finally pull away, both of their faces are moist with tears.

Unsure as to how to act, Leslie cowers somewhere in the distance. In all of this time that I've known her, I've never seen her so afraid. The confident, assertive woman seems to vanish before my eyes.

But then Harley surprises me. Instead of questioning her or bringing up the past, she walks over and gives her a warm hug.

They hold each other for a few minutes as the rest of us watch. Harold smiles at me. An expression of relief sweeps over his face. Everything is going to be alright now, he probably wants to say.

"I was so worried," Leslie says, kissing Harley's cheek as if she were a child.

"I'm fine," Harley mumbles.

"I know. I'm just so...relieved that everything worked out. It was so scary."

"Yeah, tell me about it," Harley jokes, but it doesn't land.

"Hi, I'm Aurora."

Aurora extends her hand just as Leslie finally pulls away from Harley, giving her some breathing room. Everyone in the room has somehow completely forgotten that she is here, which isn't really something that ever happens to Aurora.

Harley shakes her hand and thanks her for being there for me through all of this. Clearly taken aback by her generosity, Aurora blushes.

As nice as it is to see them again, luckily, Leslie

and Harold don't stay too long. They head back to their hotel within the hour with a promise to come back tomorrow morning. Once they leave, I let out a big sigh of relief.

I didn't realize that they were going to be here and when I first saw Leslie standing in the foyer, a part of me tensed up. The last time Harley met with her mom, she left angry and discontented. Her mother had tricked her and brought her out to Montana and then tried to make amends. I am certain that Harley isn't necessarily over this little misstep but at least she has chosen to let it go for tonight.

And then it's just the three of us. Aurora asks us if we want anything to eat, but Harley shakes her head and yawns. Aurora takes the hint boiling some water for her tea and retires to the guest room.

Finally, it's just us.

I take Harley into my arms and wrap them tightly around her waist. I want to carry her up the stairs and take off all of her clothes. But when she looks up at me, I know that tonight's not a good night for that. Rings of exhaustion circle her eyes and she yawns again and again.

"Come on, let's go to bed," I whisper, helping her up the stairs.

My room is exactly as I left it and that gives me the comfort that I'm craving. Harley is still finding it difficult to walk given how damaged her feet were in the snow overnight, but she doesn't let me pick her up until we get right up to the bed. Then she leans on me, letting her body go limp and falls into my arms. I carefully place her on the bed and pull the comforter along with the sheet on top of her. Before I can reach over and kiss her on the cheek, she turns away, folds herself in two, and falls asleep.

EVEN THOUGH MY body is exhausted and spent, my mind continues to race and I know that I won't be able to fall asleep. Instead, I turn off the main lights and flip on two electronic candles. Then I climb into bed and watch her sleep.

Time comes to a standstill and I lose myself in her steady breathing. Having her here with me, safe and unharmed, I finally allow my mind to go to that dark place that I could not cope with before. What if this hadn't turned out the way it did? What would I do if she had been hurt? What would I do if she had been killed?

Looking back, Harley's death seems like a real

possibility. It is not every day that women who find themselves in her situation are able to get out alive. But she did. But what if she hadn't? What if instead of sitting here and watching her breathe, I had to go to her funeral?

What if, like my sweet Lila, she returned to dust from which she came from? I don't think I could survive something like that.

When I lost Lila, I left my life behind and became a recluse. I had contemplated suicide and even gone as far as to tie a rope around the beam in the dining room. The only thing that stopped me was holding Lila's ashes in my hands and knowing that if she went somewhere that people say we go after we die then she would be looking down at me at this moment with disappointment. I knew that Lila would want me to keep living my life despite what happened to her. And so would Harley, of course. But if I had lost her at this point in my life… after I had lost my only child, well, I doubt that I would have much of a reason to keep going.

HARLEY

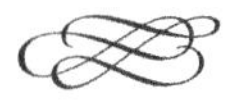

WHEN HE KISSES ME...

I wake up a few hours later and stare at him as he sleeps. Not entirely convinced that I'm not dreaming, I reach to Jackson and touch him on the arm. Being a light sleeper, he stirs in his sleep and opens his eyes.

"I'm sorry, I didn't mean to wake you." I gasp, covering my mouth with my hand.

"It's fine," he yawns.

"How are you?"

His yawn makes me yawn.

"Ready to go back to sleep?" Jackson asks sleepily. I shrug and shake my head. Then I lean over to him, placing my mouth on his.

"Oh...I see...you have something else in mind," he jokes.

As we kiss, my tiredness seems to vanish. It's quickly replaced by another emotion that courses through my body.

For a moment, I pull away and look at him straight on. His movements are confident and sexy. His eyes are ablaze. My heart starts to beat so loud that it sounds as if someone were pounding on a drum kit with all of their might.

"Let's get these clothes off," he says, tugging at my shirt. But then he reaches for my mouth again and our arms and legs intertwine. I wrap my legs around his torso, pressing him as tightly as possible. He reciprocates by moving his hips in such a way that makes me dizzy.

"I want you," he whispers into my ear.

"I want you, too." My breath quickens. I watch as he sits up and pulls my shirt over my head. When my body bounces back onto the bed, he gets off me and pulls off my pants. I'm not wearing a bra, but I am still wearing a pair of panties. Running his fingers along the top, just below my hip bones, he makes my whole body burn for his. Just as I am about to pull off my underwear, he flips me over and slides them down, pressing his mouth to my butt cheeks.

Once my body is free of all clothing, he spreads

my legs and thrusts his fingers deep inside of me. I moan from the pleasure. The muscles deep inside of me clench up and then relax with each move.

"Don't move," he instructs, keeping one hand where it is and taking off his clothes with the other. When he needs the one inside of me, he simply switches.

Once his body is free of clothing, he climbs on top of me and gives me light, feather-like kisses on top of my shoulders. His movements start to slow down along with my breathing. But then, suddenly, he buries his hand in my hair and tugs. Hard.

"Ah," I moan into the pillow. The sensation of my hair being pulled sends chills down my body. With my neck turned toward one side, he presses his lips to mine. His kiss is sloppy and demanding and I like how messy and primal it feels. His tongue and lips coax mine. When I moan, I moan straight into his mouth and our tongues intertwine.

With his body draped on top of mine, we move as one, but I want more. I want him inside of me.

"Come on, stop teasing," I say into the pillow.

"Oh...you want more?"

"Of course, don't you?"

I want him so badly that I ache for him. I flip over to my back and bring my hands up to his face.

Then into his hair. It's soft and wild. The large thick curls look like they are consuming his face. When I bury my hands in it, he moans and then groans. But then pulls away.

"Where are you going?" I demand to know before I realize his intentions. He is traveling south. With one swift move, he grabs my hips and runs his tongue around my belly button, kissing the top of each hip bone, before traveling further down.

"Ahhh," I moan, burying my hands further in his locks. My body seems to start moving on its own as his tongue finds my center. His fingers make their way back inside and after a few more swirls, the warm sensation building up in my core starts to creep to the surface.

"You taste so...good," he mumbles in between his kisses. Now, I'm not so much moaning as panting.

"I'm getting close," I whisper through the pleasure. And suddenly, he stops.

"No, not yet."

"Oh, no, please!" I plead and try to push his hands back inside of me. But Jackson just laughs.

Leaning over me, he whispers, "Get on your hands and knees."

A jolt of electricity rushes through me. I do as he says and wait. He moves slightly away and examines me. Normally, this would make me shy away and get really self-conscious, but I am too aroused to feel anything but desire.

He runs his fingers down my spine and over my butt cheeks. Then he slowly repositions my legs, opening them wider. I arch my back from anticipation. My whole body is screaming for his.

Finally, it's time. He gets behind me and slowly pushes himself inside. My body envelopes him and we start to move as one.

I don't last long. I am too turned on to wait any longer. I need a release. When I feel a warm soothing sensation build somewhere deep inside of me, I bury my face in the pillow and scream his name.

HARLEY

WHEN I WAKE UP…

When I wake up in his arms the following morning, everything is back in place. The world is just as it's supposed to be. Jackson is lying next to me. His chest rises up and down with each breath and his face is calm and peaceful. The tension that existed there before is gone, hopefully not to return for a very long time.

I get out of bed and walk toward the terrace. It's cold outside and I have no intention of bundling up and going out there. The room is a toasty seventy-eight degrees and I feel comfortable walking around in my bare feet dressed in nothing but a t-shirt. The world outside is gray and in mourning, but I'm not. For the first time in a long time, I feel truly happy. In this room, I have everything that I want. I am free in every way that a person can be free and after being held hostage, this feeling is pure ecstasy.

I walk over to the desk facing the other side of the street and open the computer. It's Jackson's private laptop, so there's no password to get in. I log into my email and delete over two hundred pieces of spam and other things of no interest. The one that remains is from Amazon.

The subject line reads, *Your book is now available in the Kindle Store.*

It's an old email that I had completely forgotten about. Actually, I had forgotten about my book completely.

I log into Kindle Direct Publishing and click on Reports.

Oh my God!

I look at the bar graph showing how many units were ordered each of the last few days. Am I reading this correctly?

The first day I had three sales. Then five. Then eight and six.

I head to the main site and search for my book. It now has six reviews! All five stars except for one, which is four.

People are actually reading this book? I stare at the dashboard in disbelief.

"Hey." Jackson gives me a kiss on the top of my head. I was so engrossed in my results that I didn't hear him get up at all.

"Look at this!" I say excitedly.

"So, people are buying your book?"

I nod.

"Told ya."

I roll my eyes.

"I'm really proud of you."

We both stare at the bar graph for a moment. When I refresh the page, I have another sale.

"How are they finding it?"

I shrug.

"Did you do any marketing?"

I shake my head.

"So, this is without any advertising at all?"

I nod.

"What about social media? Did you post stuff there?"

"No. I published it under another name because...well, it's very sexy and I wasn't sure where this whole thing was going to go."

Jackson gives me a look that says, I understand. There's no need to explain.

I don't know if publishing this book under a pseudonym was the right thing to do, but it certainly feels like it. The thing is that it's hard to put yourself out there. It's hard to try something new and there's a really big fear of failure that comes with every attempt. At least, on my part. And this fear is especially prominent when it comes to my writing.

It's so easy for people to dismiss a book as stupid or badly written, but as a writer you can't help but take that sort of thing personally. These are your words that these critics are marring and it's your blood, sweat, and tears that they are tossing aside as insignificant. It's not that everyone has to love what I do. Of course not. There are plenty of books that I don't like and wouldn't recommend to others.

But the problem with writing a love story, and especially a romance, is that everyone out there in the so-called 'real world' is all too quick to dismiss these books as shit. Readers devour romance books and historically it is books about love that stand the test of time. E. L. James has sold more books than the Bible and people all over the world have devoured them with great appetites and yet critics and 'serious' readers consider them trash.

Perhaps it is cowardly of me to use another name to publish my words, but it's the only way I could see to do it. But it is not just the critics that I'm afraid of. There's something else as well. This book has a lot of steamy scenes which I, and other readers, love. They are tame in comparison to some that I've read before, but to people who haven't read much in this genre, they will undoubtably be risqué.

"So, your book is about me, right? Or rather us?" Jackson asks after he comes out of the shower. "I mean, reclusive billionaire meets a virgin?"

My heart jumps into my throat. I had no idea he knew.

"I looked it up on Amazon. Sounds like a great read."

"So...you're not mad?" I ask.

"No, not at all. I mean, you're not even using your real name. Who's going to know?"

"It's not really about us. I mean, it is on the surface. But even the sexy scenes aren't really anything like ours."

"Oh, no, well, we're going to have to fix that," he says, taking me into his arms. Our mouths collide and our tongues intertwine. His lips are soft and effervescent, yet strong and demanding.

"So...it's really okay?" I ask. "I mean, this whole thing is...sort of stressing me out."

"Why?"

I shrug. "I have never put myself out there like

this before. I mean, I did with the blog, and you saw how well that turned out."

Jackson shakes his head and kisses me again. "You have every right to tell whatever story you want to tell. If you want to write about us, that's fine. If you want to make it a bit of the truth and a whole lot of fiction, that's fine, too. It's your novel. You're the writer. Please don't ever apologize for your imagination. It's one of the most beautiful things about you."

My heart skips a beat. And then another and another. I've never felt such support before. To write is to bare yourself completely to the whole world and that requires a very thick skin. I've learned that through my blog. But back then what made things so difficult was that I didn't have this support. I didn't have someone in my corner cheering me on. It makes having thick skin a lot easier, because when something does happen, you don't bruise as much.

"So, what are your plans to market this baby?"

HARLEY

WHEN HE TEACHES ME ABOUT MARKETING...

I'm not entirely sure what Jackson means by market. He looks at me surprised.

"So, you're just planning on putting it out there and not doing anything to tell people about it?"

I shrug. "I'm not entirely sure what I can do."

"Well, actually, you can do a lot."

I listen as Jackson dives into the details of online marketing. I don't know a thing about it but I'm eager to learn. The organic sales that I managed to scrounge up are wonderful, of course, but the idea of actually bringing my book to the masses makes the little hairs on the back of my arms stand up.

Jackson tells me that I should start new Facebook and Instagram accounts which are devoted just to my author brand. Brand? Wow, suddenly, this whole thing sounds very legitimate.

"Then you'll be able to tell your friends and followers about your new books and releases, and whatever personal things you want to share."

I nod.

"In addition, you should also start an exclusive Facebook group just for your readers."

"Who's going to join that?"

"Well, it will start out small but it will gain momentum as you publish more books."

More books? Of course, I've considered continuing the story. It even ends on somewhat of a cliffhanger, but publish more? So soon?

"The thing about online content is that people just want more and more of it. As long as you can maintain quality, the way to build your brand is to publish as much and as often as you can. That means you'll have to do a lot of work."

"I'm not worried about that. I'd love to just write for a living. But will people really read it?"

"I've done some research into this category and series do really well. So, if you're willing to commit to this, then the best advice is to keep going."

I tap my foot on the floor, largely out of excitement.

"But writing isn't the only thing you will need to do. You also have to capture people's email addresses. Email marketing is still one of the most important ways that people sell things online and readers want to hear from you. They want to know when you have a new book out. Once you set up a newsletter using Mailerlite or Mailchimp or another mass email service, then make sure to share your link on your Facebook page and group as well as inside the back cover of your book."

The information coming out of Jackson's mouth hits me like an avalanche and I pick up a piece of paper and a pen and start to take notes. He gives me a moment to write down what he has just said and then continues with the lecture.

"All of these social media strategies are effective and necessary, but the main way that you will find new readers is through Facebook ads."

"Ads? What do you mean?"

"I'm sure that you've seen those sponsored ads on your Facebook feed when you scroll. Those are all paid advertising and, targeted correctly to the right audience, they are very effective in resulting in sales."

"But how do I learn to do them? I don't know anything about them."

Jackson shrugs. "Once you set up all of your social media and the newsletter and the group then I'll show you how to create them and tailor them to your books. They are not very difficult to figure out and there're a million different courses and videos about them on Udemy and YouTube. So you can either watch those or I can show you, or both if you really want to learn the nitty gritty."

As he talks, I type in 'how to make effective Facebook ads' into the search bar and discover that he's right.

"Wow, this is so exciting," I whisper under my breath. "It's going to be a lot of work but the idea that I can actually help readers find out about my books. Well, that's...everything."

Jackson gives me a kiss on the cheek.

"It's so great to see you so inspired."

And then, suddenly, something occurs to me.

"Wait, but Facebook ads require money. How much do they cost?"

"What makes them so effective is that there isn't one blanket price. It's all about your targeting and how much it costs for a particular person to click on this ad. Not all of them will convert, but typically you want to aim for as low a cost per click as possible."

"And what does a click cost?"

"Under twenty cents per click is pretty good. But again, it depends entirely on your audience, targeting, and the design of the ad. Besides testing the image and the copy of the ad, even things like the headline and the specific style of copy will have a big impact on click and conversion."

None of this really makes any sense to me but I'm pretty certain that I can probably figure it out.

"So, how much money will I have to spend a day?"

"Whatever you want really. Or whatever you think the book can support. The good thing is that you don't have to start out with much. You can just set up to spend at five or ten dollars a day and do your testing and then increase it as you start to see sales."

That sounds good except that there's one problem. And it's a big one.

"What's wrong?"

"I don't really have any money to pay for this."

HARLEY

WHEN I GET TO WORK...

Ten dollars a day doesn't sound like much, but that's three hundred dollars a month. The kind of money that I don't really have to spare. Not now, not anytime soon.

Jackson waits for me to answer, but I don't want to borrow more money from him. He is paying for everything and it doesn't feel good to not be able to contribute at all.

"I can give you the money," Jackson says. "Please don't worry about that."

I look away from him.

"What's wrong? It's really not that much."

I can't believe that he just said that to me.

"Yeah, I know that it feels like that to you. But it's... a lot for me."

"That's not what I meant at all. I mean, that my money is your money."

When I look up at him, I realize that he really doesn't know what he's saying.

"But it's not really. It's your money. And that's fine. I don't want any of it. I'm just trying to explain... why I can't do certain things."

Jackson shakes his head.

"You already live a pretty frugal life, Harley. But businesses require investment. And don't you think that what you're doing now is starting a business?"

I don't understand what he's saying.

"Traditional writers have the luxury of just sitting back and allowing their publisher to take care of all their marketing expenses. But that's one of the reasons why so few of them make any money. There's a lot of money to be made in indie publishing but in order to do so you have to approach it like a business."

"What does that mean?" I ask after a moment.

"In addition to writing a lot of books, you have to spend time marketing your work. You need to keep finding new readers and that's the only way that you can make this a successful career."

"So...I have to invest in Facebook ads?"

"It's the easiest way to find new readers. So, why the hell not?"

I shake my head again.

"I know that you are proud, but I really want to help you. And it's not that much money for me. So, why don't you let me pay for it?"

I take a deep breath. He's right, of course. Maybe I am stupid not to, or just too prideful, or a bit of both.

"I know that it's important to invest in the business...I just don't feel right taking your money, okay?"

Jackson nods and pulls me closer to him.

"I love you, Harley. The last thing that I want to do is to make you feel uncomfortable in any way. I just want you to know that I'm here for you. No matter what."

"I appreciate that," I whisper and kiss him back.

THIS MORNING I have a bit of time to myself as Jackson goes to another room to get some work done. I don't know what to really do so I decide to get started on some of the marketing tasks for my author 'brand.' That word 'brand' sounds silly to me. I mean, who the hell am I to have a brand? But if I want readers to find my books and I want to really do this on my own, I guess that's exactly what it requires.

The initial parts of the process are not so much hard as tedious. I already have a pseudonym, Nicole Woodhouse, and I set up all the necessary social media for that name. Within half an hour, Nicole Woodhouse exists as a real person. I re-write my author bio and include those accounts in it. Then I turn to Mailerlite and set up an account for my newsletter. Apparently, you can't use regular email accounts like Google or Yahoo to email a lot of people at once because they will flag it as spam. So, there are other email services there that are meant for companies who want to communicate with their customers.

Jackson didn't mention much about setting up an author website, but I figure that I will need that as well. I look into a few service providers like Squarespace and Wordpress. I don't know anything about making websites and the Wordpress site seems too particularly daunting as a result. So, I put this to the side for a moment and decide to watch some videos on the thing that scares me the most; Facebook advertising.

It's difficult to describe what it is about paid advertising that makes me so uneasy but it has something to do with the fact that I know very little about it. The whole process requires me to write the copy and design an image as well as figure out targeting and optimize the ads. In addition to these creative aspects, there are also more technical requirements as well. I have to figure out how to use Facebook Ads manager, and how to physically set up the advertisements within the architecture. And then, of course, there are the financial particulars. Ten dollars a day doesn't sound like much, but it really adds up. And the results? They're not really guaranteed.

I take a deep breath and click on the first YouTube video that explains the layout of the Ads Manager. As the host walks me through it, I connect my new Nicole Woodhouse Facebook page to the manager and follow along. Within a few minutes, this aspect of it is demystified.

That's the funny thing about education, isn't it? At first, the problem seems impossible to solve. And the more you think about it, the more anxiety and tension you get. But after just a little bit of research, everything starts to fall into place. You quickly realize that if these people in these videos can figure it out, then you can as well. At least, that's how I've always felt.

By the time Jackson comes back to the room about two hours later, I have a firm grasp on what I need to do and how to do it. Even though I still don't know what exactly would make for good copy and an image for my book, I know how I can make it. I don't know much about graphic design but one of the YouTubers recommended a program called Canva, which allows you to simply drag and drop images. It seems pretty easy to use and they have many different templates including ones for book covers, social media posts of various sizes, as well as Facebook ads.

"Wow, you're not wasting much time, are you?" Jackson says as I go over everything that I have accomplished this morning.

I shake my head no.

"I've never been one to procrastinate much, especially when working on a project that really excites me."

That's one of the qualities that I'm most proud of, actually. Once I focus on something even if I'm afraid to do it, I will really put in a lot of work to accomplish it.

"Well, I think you have worked very hard and you deserve a break."

He walks over and places his hands on my shoulders and begins to rub them.

"Wow, you are very tense. We are going to have to figure out some way to work out some of this tension."

As his capable hands focus on the knots right below my neck, shivers of pleasure run down my spine. I tilt my head forward and let my hair fall into my face.

HARLEY

WHEN WE ARE INTERRUPTED...

Jackson traces circles with his tongue, leaving goose bumps in his wake. My body starts to shiver in anticipation. He pulls me out of my seat and into his arms. His hands run down my back and make themselves comfortable on my butt. I run my fingers down his chest and pick at the top button. It opens easily, leading me to the next and the next.

I don't even notice the burns anymore. His skin is bumpy and scarred all the way down his front, but I touch it as if it were smooth. It's a part of him and the only thing that repulses me about it is the pain that he went through to endure this.

The other thing that's different now is his own response to my touch. At first, he cowered away, self-conscious of his imperfections (his words, not mine). He had told me how disgusted others had been when he showed them his burns. Their responses make me sick to my stomach. When I look at him, all I see is beauty. My heart goes out to him for what he has been through, but other than that nothing about his scars bothers me.

I run my fingers down to his navel. His pants hang low on his hips, exposing his hip bones and the muscles that make a V, going down to his groin. They flex, revealing a perfect six-pack as he moves, and my mouth salivates.

When we make our way to the bed, he pushes me down and gets on top of me. My whole body tenses up in anticipation as my mouth intertwines with his.

Suddenly, the doorbell goes off. We pause and listen.

"Who could that be?" I ask. The expression on his face falls. I narrow my eyes.

"What?" I demand to know.

"Your parents. I forgot that they were coming over."

The doorbell rings again. Jackson gives me a kiss and pulls me up, against my will.

"No...let's just pretend we're not home," I moan.

"They'll be worried."

I roll my eyes, knowing full well that that's exactly what will happen.

A moment later, my phone beeps and so does his.

He picks it up and quickly texts back, *coming*.

Jackson holds my hand all the way down the stairs and toward the front door, and only lets go when it's time to say hello.

I hug my mom again just like I did last night. Our embrace is warm and genuine, reminding me of how it used to feel to have her in my arms. Somehow, the anger and the hurt that I felt the last time I saw her vanishes and I all I want is to go back to the way things were.

As we sit down around the kitchen island and Jackson starts to make everyone coffee and breakfast, I marvel at how not weird it feels to be with them again. Somehow, everything that happened in Montana doesn't seem to matter anymore. It's not that I have forgotten about it, but being with them now, I don't really care about that.

Over breakfast, we sit and talk about nothing at all. I guess they are waiting for me to bring up the kidnapping, but I'd rather enjoy this moment and focus on something else. I'm not avoiding it on purpose. It just doesn't pop into my head until hours later. Instead, we spend the time getting to know each other again. I ask my mom about work and she catches me up on what has been going on. Not the cases, but her colleagues.

"Marcy is pregnant again. It's going to be her sixth baby," Mom says. Marcy is a detective and one of Mom's closest friends.

"Oh my God." I laugh. "How the hell does she have time for that? Or the energy? Does she ever sleep?"

"I don't think so."

"Dan is getting married."

"To whom?"

"That girl from Thailand."

"Wait, what?"

"Oh, you don't know. Of course, why would you?" Mom laughs. "Yeah, after his divorce he swore off American women and went on this month long trip to Southeast Asia. And that's where he met her."

"Wow." I shake my head. "Have you met her?"

"Yeah, actually, she seems really nice."

"She looks about eighteen," Dad says.

"But she's not. She's in her thirties, just like him. I think she might be a few years older than him, actually."

Jackson and I exchange smiles. I'm not sure exactly what his smile means, but I'm smiling because it's just so nice to be with them again. And have it be normal. Like it was before, when they were happy.

"So, what about you?" Jackson asks. "You're back together, right?"

My parents look at each other like love-struck teenagers.

"Actually—" my mom says, her eyes twinkling.

"What?"

"Your father asked me to marry him."

I look at Dad, who places his arm on her shoulders and gives her a big wide kiss.

The news catches me a bit off guard, almost knocking the wind out of me. I feel blood draining away from my face.

"Are you okay?" Jackson whispers in my ear while my parents are locked in their kiss.

I give him a little nod. No, I'm not really okay, but I don't want to put a damper on the moment. Instead, I force a little smile and congratulate them.

It's not that I'm not happy for them or that I don't see how in love they are again. It's just that their divorce was one of the darkest moments in my life. For a long time, I had wished they would get over their differences and get back together. And then for an even longer time, I had wished that they would learn to be content being divorced. I thought that this moment would fill me with joy but something is holding me back.

HARLEY

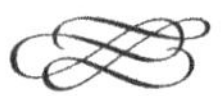

WHEN I MAKE AMENDS...

"I know you have your concerns, Harley," Dad says, without moving his arm off Mom's shoulder. "But we are in love. We've always been in love, actually. It's just that we went through so much that we thought that we would be better apart."

I nod.

"But we're not," Mom says.

"What's wrong?" Dad asks. "What's with that sad expression?"

I take a deep breath. I guess I have to tell them. If I want to start a new relationship with them, I can't pretend that everything is fine and then stew in my own anger. I can't keep my feelings bottled up.

"I'm just a little concerned," I start. I don't know

exactly how to put any of this into words, let alone delicate words that won't hurt their feelings. But I have to try.

"You look happy. And I know that you are happy in this moment, but I'm just wondering if you are moving too fast."

Dad shakes his head.

"I've loved this woman more than half of my life, Harley. She has been my world. And I know that we have been through our share of problems. But none of them were really internal problems. It wasn't our personalities that clashed. It wasn't like we weren't getting along."

He's right. I know that. I remember how happy they were before. They rarely fought or had any sort of disagreements. It wasn't until I was in high school that I realized that married couples even argued about anything.

"It was one particular instance that drove us apart," Mom says. She doesn't mention Aspen by name and I appreciate that.

"I know that it lasted for a while, but it all stemmed from that fire."

I clench my fists when I hear that word, bracing myself for the memories that are going to flood through me.

"I don't want to talk about that, honey," Mom says, grabbing my hand and bringing me back to the present. "All I want to say is that maybe we shouldn't have let everything that happened push us apart. But that's life, right? You can't really go back in time and change things; you can only learn from it."

I nod. Her hand feels nice in mine. It's soft and warm and comforting. It's the hand that taught me how to walk and how to drive. It's the hand that I remember from childhood.

"And as long as we're talking about regrets, let me tell you how much I regret what I did to bring you back to Montana," she whispers.

Her voice is cracking and tears are forming around the bottom of her eyes. My mom rarely cries and it takes all of my strength to push my own tears away to no avail.

"I shouldn't have done that. I should've come here to New York and found you. I was a coward for orchestrating all of that. And I hope that you will find it in your heart to forgive me."

All I can do is nod as tears roll down my cheeks. I wipe them off, but they are quickly replaced by new ones. Finally, when I am somewhat able to get control of myself, I whisper, "I forgive you," and wrap my arms around her.

We hold each other for a few moments and when we pull away, it's like none of that ever happened. I know that we will never speak of this again.

"Do you give us your blessing, honey?" Dad asks.

I take a deep breath. The more I think about this, the more I realize that it's not the fact that they are getting married again that will be a mistake, but it's rather that they got divorced in the first place. That was the thing that never should've happened.

"Yes, of course," I say and my parents throw their arms around me. After a moment, Dad pulls Jackson in on the family hug as well.

"So, what kind of wedding do you want to have?" I ask after the level of emotion in the room diminishes tenfold.

Mom and Dad exchange mischievous looks.

"What? What is that? What are you planning?" I laugh.

"We'd like to do it here. In New York."

"Really?" I ask. "But you've never really been here before."

"You made this place your home," Dad says. "And you and Jackson had a lot to do with bringing us back together. So, we'd like to do it here if you don't mind."

Jackson smiles widely, putting his arm around me. He gives me a big squeeze.

"Yes, of course," we say, almost simultaneously.

When my parents leave later that afternoon for a trip to the Museum of Modern Art, I plop down on the couch in front of the fire where we first talked and lose myself in the flames.

"Are you okay?" Jackson asks, sitting down next to me. I take his hand in mine.

"Yes."

We watch the fire for a few moments without saying a word.

"I'm just feeling so...serene."

I'm not sure if that's the right word to describe the day, but it's the only one that comes to mind.

"It's hard to explain, but it's only now that I realize how much weight I have been carrying around over their relationship. And now, knowing that they are happy and are getting re-married...that weight has been lifted off my shoulders. Completely."

"It makes me so happy to see you...this way," Jackson says quietly. "You do look lighter."

He snuggles up to me and places his head on the couch next to mine. Then he tilts my face toward him and kisses me. Our tongues intertwine. His lips feel strong and confident and disarming at the same time. Shivers run down my body as I bury my hands in his hair. He tugs at my shirt and pulls it up over my head. My hair falls back into my face and he moves it out of the way to see my eyes.

"You are so...beautiful," he whispers.

JACKSON

WHEN WE INTERTWINE...

My craving for Harley is location independent. It doesn't matter whether we are in bed, on the plane, in a cabin, or here on this couch where we first met, my body needs her in the same way it needs oxygen.

I clutch her and wrap her around me, taking nourishment from her breaths. She presses her body to mine and slips her warm hand under the front of my shirt.

I tighten and relax my calf muscles, trying to calm their restlessness. But it's to no avail. I'm hungry for her. Tilting her chin to the ceiling, I run my fingers down the curvature of her neck. Her hair falls in waves behind her and she licks her plump little lips. Quickly, a serene smile emerges and settles comfortably on her face.

As my lips make their way down to her breasts, I close my eyes and go by feel. I have memorized the contours of her body a long time ago. Yet, I still can't get enough. Every time we are together it feels familiar and completely new at the same time.

The anticipation that I feel sends knots of electricity through my groin. I am so turned on, I am raging and throbbing for her. My heartbeat is erratic and occasionally I have to slow down and pull away to gain some breath.

Before I lean her on the couch, I take off her shirt and pull off her pants, leaving her in just a lacy pair of panties. She isn't wearing a bra and I revel in the way her breasts fall to one side and then another with each move of her body. I kneel down on the floor beside her and look at her. I know every mole and freckle on her body. She doesn't have many but the few that she does have look like they have been almost strategically placed by a higher power.

I run my fingers over the dark edges of her nipples and enjoy the way that they harden against my tongue. Her breaths speed up and I pull away to look at her again.

"What's wrong?" Harley asks, propping herself up with her elbows.

"Nothing."

"So...what are you doing?"

"I'm just admiring you."

She rolls her eyes. I know that she has her insecurities about her body, but I don't see any of the imperfections that she sees. To me, she is perfect in every possible way. To me, she is a goddess.

I run my fingers in between her thighs and then up to the mound just below her pubic bone and along the top of her panties. Her panties sit low and her hip bones rise and fall with each breath. I reach over and kiss the one that's closest to me and then move to the other one.

Suddenly, I feel like I've waited for this moment for years. It doesn't make much sense, but it's as if I have waited for her even before I knew that she existed. Is that what it's like when you find the one person who is your match? The person who is your perfect complement. There was a time when I thought that I had lost her and that part of me was hijacked. Not only did they kidnap her, but they also kidnapped a part of me.

Then, suddenly, something changes. We lunge at

each other, almost at the same time. Colliding, our lips slide over each other's and I climb on top of her. I bury my hands in the cushions and feel the tightness of her butt. My body intertwines and drapes over hers. But she pushes at me. In fact, one motion is so hard that we roll off the couch altogether.

"Oh my God, are you okay?" she whispers after I bang the back of my head on the hard wood. It's not a very hard fall, but it's significant enough to make a scene of.

"Now, you're going to have to make me feel better," I say. "You hurt me...bad."

"Okay, I think we can arrange that." Harley laughs. "But only if I can hurt you more."

"I thought that you would never ask."

She stands up for a moment and slides off her panties. Then she kneels next to me and pulls off my pants and underwear. When she opens her legs and slides on top of me. I sprawl beneath her and lose myself in the moment. As she moves her body up and down on top of me, my body gets filled with a familiar sensation of arousal. But it even goes further than that. There is something else at play here. Instead of me penetrating her, I feel like she is consuming me. Bringing me into her body and making me hers.

"Does this feel good?" she moans, moving her hips faster and faster.

"So good," I mumble. My words are barely audible.

When I feel like she is getting close, I pick her up and flip her over on her stomach. It's not that I don't want her to feel pleasure. It's that I want her to wait.

"That wasn't very nice," she says into the floor.

"I am not a very nice man."

As I slide my way inside of her again, I am rough and impatient and that makes her even louder. But still, it doesn't feel like I am in control. She is taking me inside of her. She is enveloping me. She is consuming me.

"Oh, Harley," I whisper her name as I get closer and closer. My hips move faster and faster and then suddenly hers do as well.

"Yes!" Harley's screams are muffled by the nearby throw pillow.

"Yes!" I yell at the top of my lungs.

Our bodies continue to move as one long after I collapse on top of her and cover her as if I am a blanket of flesh.

She whispers something, but I don't hear her.

"That was...amazing," she says when I pull her head away by her hair.

"Yes, yes, it was."

"Want to do it again?"

HARLEY

WHEN I TRY TO FIND OUT MORE...

Lying in his arms, drenched in sweat and still panting from what I just experienced, I look over at Jackson. His face is completely relaxed, serene even. It's not that his face is expressionless, it's more like he reached this other level that's beyond a simple pleasure or displeasure. A new level of consciousness, perhaps? Maybe I'm just reading too much into all of this.

I stare at him for a few moments waiting for him to notice, but he doesn't. Finally, I pinch him. A smile slowly appears. He is still not fully present with me, but at least he's coming back.

"Hey, where are you, Jackson?" I nudge him.

"I'm here," he says, still looking away.

"Was that good for you?"

"It was amazing. Thank you."

"No, thank *you*. I loved it."

Still lost in thought, he doesn't say anything for a few minutes. And then something occurs to me.

"So...you've always been called Jackson?"

The question catches him off guard and he turns to me. Finally, the trance is broken.

"What do you mean?"

"Like when you were a little kid...did your mom call you Jackson?"

This is my not so tactful way of asking about his parents. I hadn't considered his family much, meaning his mom and dad, before this morning really. I had such a difficult past with my own family that I didn't really want to even ask about his. But now that things are so much better, it suddenly feels like a void that I don't know anything about his.

"No. They called me Jack," he says quietly. The faraway look on his face vanishes, replaced by a concern that settles in between his eyebrows. Suddenly, he looks tense. Reserved, even.

I wait for him to continue, not wanting to pester him. But he doesn't. Instead, he reaches for his phone and starts to type something.

"What are you doing?" I ask, pulling around my shoulders.

"Texting Aurora."

My jaw clenches up. Yes, of course. The beautiful, rich, and glamorous ex-wife who just happens to be staying at his house, the one she helped pay for. Now, instead of learning more about who he is, I have to dwell on her. Isn't that perfect? I think to myself sarcastically.

"Why?"

"She's not here."

I shrug.

"I'm just wondering where she is, that's all."

After shooting the text, he puts his phone down and looks at me. He can't see my face but I know that despite my best efforts, my face has contorted into some sort of sour expression.

Why do you care? Why are you bringing her into this moment? In our bed? These are the questions that I want to scream at him, but I bite my tongue. I'm not one to throw a fit, I'm much better at sighing and showing my displeasure in a more subtle way.

But he doesn't seem to catch on to my signals. He gives me a peck on the cheek and pulls on a pair of pants.

I take a deep breath and change the topic.

"So, are you really not going to tell me about your parents?" I ask bluntly.

Surprised, he shrugs his shoulders.

"Not really sure what to tell you."

"Well, I don't know anything, so you could start there."

"Are you okay, Harley? I mean, did I do something wrong?"

I shake my head. He leans closer to me and I can't help but kiss him. But this only confuses the situation.

"No, not at all. I was just wondering about your name and then I thought about your parents and how I don't know anything about them."

"You didn't seem to care before," he points out.

"Yeah, well, hanging out with my own and making amends and everything just sort of put things in perspective."

He nods, buttoning his shirt. I grab my own panties and jeans and pull them on, keeping myself covered by the sheet which he brought from the bed. He laughs.

"Shut up!" I say, turning away from him and putting on my long sleeve V-neck without bothering with a bra.

He walks up to me and grabs me by my waist, spinning me around toward him.

"You have an *amazing* body, and don't you dare think anything bad about it."

His words warm my heart, but they don't really change how I feel. That's the thing about self-perception. You may look amazing on the outside, but it's how you perceive yourself that impacts your truth about yourself. I may not be a big girl by society's standards, but there are a lot of things about my body that I am insecure about. I know that now everyone says to love yourself, no matter what, but that's not that easy to accomplish. Loving yourself unconditionally takes a lot of patience and hard work and I haven't been devoted to either.

Jackson leans me back and kisses my lips as he dips me. His mouth starts out on my lips but then quickly makes it way down my neck and to the top of my heaving breasts. There, he remains. Even as I stand straight up, he continues to caress and play with my chest. My breathing quickens as I try to push him away, but he refuses to take no for an answer. It's all for fun. I'm not really pushing him away and he's not really fighting me on this. It's a game we play and it makes us both very excited. But his hands travel south, and I suck in my stomach and suddenly the mood of the moment changes.

Of all people, I know that he is the one who

really understands how I feel. Though in many ways his body is much more perfect than mine, his burns eat away at his self-esteem. And no matter how much I love them or how much I tell him that he is beautiful nevertheless, I know that there are walls within him that are keeping my words out.

After he pulls away, Jackson stares into my eyes and asks, "So, what do you want to know about my parents?"

JACKSON

WHEN I TELL HER ABOUT MY PAST...

I knew this moment was coming, but I thought that it wouldn't come so fast. Harley has asked about my parents. I don't really know how to explain, but I also don't want to push her away. She's asking now because I helped her make up with her own family and that got her thinking. I take a take a deep breath and decide to tell the truth. The whole truth.

"What do you want to know about them?" I ask her again.

"Anything. Everything. Who are they? Where are they?"

I stare at her for a moment.

"Are you in touch with them?" Harley asks. "I'm

sorry...maybe, it's not my place to ask. I was just...wondering."

Of course, it's her place to ask. The problem is that it's difficult to answer.

"Yes, I am still in touch with them," I say after a moment.

"Oh, good."

I nod.

"It's just that you've never mentioned them before."

"I have one brother and my parents are still married," I say after a moment. She waits for me to continue.

"The reason that I haven't mentioned them before is that our relationship is quite difficult to talk about."

I keep circling the story without really saying anything. I'm searching for a way to explain my family in a way that would make sense to an outsider. The thing is that my parents were very disappointed by my decision to leave public life. And not just public life, but life in general. At first, they were very upset by what happened to Lila, but then they couldn't understand why I couldn't keep living my life. They couldn't understand why I became a recluse and how that was the only way I could really survive those years after I lost her.

I tell Harley this and she listens and nods as if she understands.

"The thing is that after a while, about a year into my...mourning...they sort of gave me an ultimatum. They said that they would not stay in touch with me or continue to support my behavior as long as I pushed the world away from me."

Harley shakes her head.

"So, what happened?"

"What happened is that they sort of allowed me to go deeper and deeper into this trance in this house. After I stopped talking to them, all I did was work and avoid the world outside. No one at work could really push me to engage with anyone since they all worked for me, so I was left on my own."

What I don't tell her is that this period of my life felt a lot like I was descending into a world of addiction. All I wanted was to be with my drug called loneliness and when they stopped fighting for me, stopped trying to remind me that there's this whole other world out there, the drug just swallowed me whole. I didn't stand a chance.

"So...what about now?" she asks. "You aren't a recluse now."

I take a deep breath. "I've been thinking about that actually."

"You have?"

"Yeah, I've been thinking of reaching out again."

"Were you ever close?"

"Yes, a long time ago."

"What did they do for a living?"

"They're both artists."

"Wow," she says, surprised. "I wasn't expecting that."

I shrug. "We never had much money growing up, but that didn't bother them much. Actually, we even lived in a bus for about a year when I was a teenager. A converted bus, it was more like an RV, a recreational vehicle."

"Really?" Her eyes light up. "I've always wanted to live in an RV!"

Now, it's my turn to be surprised.

"Now, let me ask you a question. How cool was it? Was it just a bit cool or was it totally awesome?" she asks, laughing. Her exuberance makes me smile.

"Most people do not have that reaction when I tell them. Aurora, for one, was horrified."

"I'm not like most people," she says, shrugging. "Now, answer my question."

Actually, looking back on that time when I lived

in a converted van brings joy into my heart. My parents just woke up one day and said that they were planning on buying a bus and converting it into a mini-house. I always thought they were really impulsive, but then I learned that they had already talked this through a few months before to make sure they really wanted to do it. That was how they were. Whatever crazy idea popped into their heads, they would mull it over for a bit and then announce it to the world.

My brother is three years younger than I am and the four of us spent all spring fixing it up and making it ours. My parents slept on a queen-size bed on one side of the bus and my brother and I each had a small sleeping nook on the other side. We made our areas quite private by building in curtains and other fixtures. And the rule was that he wasn't allowed in my area and I wasn't allowed in his.

As I share all of this with Harley, I feel my heart jumping up and down with excitement. I hadn't thought about that moment in a very long time.

"How was the trip? Where did you go?"

"A lot of places. We started in Pennsylvania, where we lived, and went across, dipping into Canada and then all the way to Alaska and the

Yukon. Then we swung south, along the coast all the way to Seattle and eventually Baja, California."

"Wow, that must've been one hell of a trip."

"I'll never forget it."

"But didn't you say you were never in Montana before?"

"No, I wasn't. We mainly traveled around Canada and then up into the north and then down along the other coast. It's funny, but we never made it to the Mountain West."

"What made them stop?"

"Actually, the bus broke down a few times and then they ran low on money. They needed to do some more commissioned work and they needed studio space for that. So, they decided to rent an apartment right where we broke down."

"Where was that?"

"Right outside of Tucson, Arizona."

"I've never been there."

"We should go. It's amazing. The saguaro cacti are so tall and there's sand everywhere. It's just ...this beautiful desert, it's so gorgeous, it will make your heart ache."

JACKSON

WHEN I TELL HER MORE ABOUT MY PAST...

It's hard to describe how excited I am by the fact that Harley is so open to my past. It wasn't like I had much to hide, but it's still nice to have her show genuine interest in it rather than just be horrified by my irresponsible parents and their poor decisions.

"So, what happened then?" Harley asks.

"Well, my brother and I were both homeschooled until I went to college, and we lived in Tucson for a year and then they bought an actual RV. This time it didn't break down and we traveled down to Mexico and Central America."

"Wow." She takes a step back. "I never knew that...people did that."

"Oh, they do, for sure. You should check out

some 'van life' people on YouTube. There are a ton and they are definitely living their best lives. They don't have much money but that's the thing about life on the road. You don't really need that much. Or at least, a lot less than you would think."

She nods and then scrunches up her face, tilting her head.

"What?" I ask.

"I just don't get it. I mean, how did you end up being Jackson Ludlow?"

"Oh, you mean, given this unorthodox upbringing, I should be out there doing crazy things?"

She nods with a smile.

"Yeah, maybe you're right. I finished high school at thirteen and then took a bunch of university courses, but I knew that the thing that I wanted to experience was a normal college experience. You know, living in a dorm. Things like that. So, that's when my parents and I parted ways. When I went to the University of North Carolina."

"How was that?"

"Not particularly challenging because I'd already taken many of those courses, but I tried to do my best. I majored in History and spent most of my time learning about other things."

She knows the rest of the story of how a little blog I started became Minetta Media.

As we talk, I feel us drifting from the original conversation. Eventually, Harley notices as well and brings us back.

"So…where are they now? When was the last time you spoke to them?"

"I haven't spoken to them in about three years. But my brother occasionally texts me and lets me know what's going on. I assume he keeps them abreast of what's going on with me, too."

She nods and looks away. It probably dawns on her about how similar our stories really are to each other. Estranged parents. Lost children. Lives changed forever by flames.

"As to where are they now," I continue. "They are living in Barcelona, Spain. They moved there a few years ago right after our rift."

"Do you want to see them again?"

I shrug and take a deep breath. The easy answer is no, I don't. It's not that I'm mad at them for rejecting me. I know that they were trying to teach me a lesson. But the thought of seeing them again just feels too much like a burden.

"I think you should," Harley says.

"Oh, really? Why is that?"

"I think it's good for you to be around people who love you."

"This coming from someone who vowed never to see her mother again."

"Yeah, well, I had a bit of an awakening."

"Only after you were kidnapped and almost killed," I say, smiling. Her face drops. I realize that I spoke out of turn.

"I'm sorry, I shouldn't have said that." I reach for her hands but she pushes me away. I try again and after a bit of resistance, she finally gives in.

"No, it's fine," Harley whispers. "I shouldn't be so...sensitive. But you're right. It did take something pretty extreme to get me to talk to my mom again and to be reminded of the mother that I had."

I smile and give her a peck on her lips.

"So...let that be a lesson."

"What do you mean?" I ask.

"Don't wait until something bad happens to reach out to them again. I mean, there was a time when you loved them. And it's not like they did anything too terrible, right?"

"Except pushing me away when I really needed them."

"But you know that they did it for your own good."

I don't want to admit it out loud, not just yet, but she's right. They were wrong to push me away and trying to influence me, but the one thing that I know is that they did it for the right reasons.

"So...how did you get so smart, anyway?" I ask.

"Well, getting kidnapped and almost killed will sober you up. Bring you back to reality, if you know what I mean."

I smile and take her into my arms again.

"And now that you're here, in this reality, what exactly do you want to do?"

"You mean, besides get you naked and stay in bed for about a week without interruption?" Harley's eyes twinkle as she speaks.

I nod, pulling her closer to me. She smells like lavender and honey and my mouth salivates just by being in her presence. I run my fingertips along her collarbone and down her side.

"I think I'd like to go to Spain."

JACKSON

WHEN THEY SHOW UP...

Did I hear that right? She wants to go to Spain?? Is she just joking or is she really serious? I stare at Harley in disbelief. She cracks a smile.

"Don't look so shocked," she says with a little shrug. "Is it really such a bad idea?"

I shake my head. I don't really know what to think.

"Look, it was just an idea. I mean, we sort of talked about getting away somewhere and what better place than Spain? You could make up with your parents. We would be away from all of this."

My whole body clenches up and I force myself to relax.

"Or you don't have to. We could just go there and...see the country."

"I'm going to get something to drink," I say and walk away from her. I grab a glass and fill it up from the tap. She follows me into the kitchen a few minutes later. But she hovers near the doorway.

"What's wrong? What did I say that was so...inappropriate?"

"Nothing. Nothing is wrong," I lie.

The truth is that her suggestion has made me defensive. When it came to her family, I tried to help her reconcile. I knew it was the right thing to do because they love her and she loves them. But when it comes to me, I have a much harder time listening to my own advice.

"Talk to me, please," Harley pleads.

I take a deep breath, collecting my thoughts.

"I know that we should make up. I mean, we never even really had a fight. They just put this ultimatum on me and I couldn't comply. Not then. For a long time, I thought that it was really unfair that they rejected me when I needed them the most. It really spiraled me further into that world. I often think, what would've happened if they had remained in my life? And I'm not sure that I would've been such a shut-in for so long."

"But it's over now," Harley says. "You're better. Your anxiety about going outside is gone, right?"

"Yeah, surprisingly. Thanks to you."

"Thanks to me bursting in and shattering your little bubble," she jokes.

"You laugh but that's what it took. I had built up all of these walls that allowed me to live the way I lived. And it wasn't until you showed up that I was forced to break out of that cocoon."

She looks up at me with her big wide eyes.

"Don't get me wrong. It was a good thing. An amazing thing. I mean, I know that night was terrible, but it was the first thing that started chipping away at all of my defenses. I wouldn't be here without you."

Harley reaches over to me, draping her arms around my neck. I pick her up and wrap her legs around my torso. We hold each other there for a few moments. Then I walk over and place her onto the kitchen island.

"I think you're right," I finally say.

"About what?"

"I think I need to get in touch with my parents again. Life is short and it's important to have people in your life that fill it with love."

Harley presses her lips onto mine.

"You fill my life with love," she whispers through our kiss.

MIDWEST PRIVATE SECURITY arrives later that afternoon. They have been highly recommended by some of the people I have reached out to and I wanted to meet them in person before making the final decision. Harley doesn't really think it's a good idea for me to hire her a bodyguard so I phrase it as us getting a security team. The truth is that it's really all about her.

Sam Davis has made a deal with the prosecutor and he will not be doing too much prison time for his drug offenses. As far as the kidnapping however, he got complete immunity for giving the police information about the whereabouts of the cabin. And as for Parker? He is still nowhere to be found. The authorities keep telling us that they are doing the best they can, but in reality, they have no idea where he is. So, their best isn't nearly good enough.

"So, what exactly would you be doing?" I ask, not entirely sure where to start. The security team consists of three people, two of whom are bodyguards and one who is the owner and the coordinator from the office.

The owner is the most burly of them all, with large muscles bulging out of his dress shirt. The bodyguards, on the other hand, aren't particularly massive, but definitely fit.

"Basically, we will be shadowing you wherever you go. If you have a specific event that you will be attending, we will first scope out the area and give you an assessment of the risks," Thomas Cockrell, the owner, says.

Harley shakes her head. Cockrell goes further into the details about various places that present specific and general risks. I appreciate all the insight, but Harley clearly doesn't. She is so annoyed that she is not even trying to hide it.

I wait until after they leave to bring it up.

"You didn't like them?" I ask.

"No, it's not that. It's just that I don't need a bodyguard."

"Harley, you were kidnapped. And almost killed. And Parker is still out there. They have no idea where he is."

"I don't care. I don't want some stranger following me around everywhere."

"I know you don't, but someone will. If we don't hire them then Parker will find you again."

Tears well up in her eyes. I hate to be so blunt, but she doesn't seem to fully understand the gravity of the situation.

"What about you?" she asks after a moment. "Why can't you be my bodyguard?"

I take a deep breath and pull her closer to me. "I'd love to. And if you want, I won't leave your side. But I just don't know everything they do, about how to protect you. You understand?"

She shakes her head no. I'm about to try to make my case again, but the doorbell rings. It's Aurora.

HARLEY

WHEN SHE ARRIVES…

I know that Aurora is staying here but still her arrival catches me by surprise. We are right in the middle of our conversation about the security team that Jackson is insisting that I need and it doesn't sound like my opinion on this matter is getting through to him.

Aurora not so much comes in the house, but flies in. She moves swiftly and excitedly around the foyer and through the kitchen, and it's clear to me that she is perfectly comfortable in her position as the woman of the house. Grabbing a salad out of the fridge and a fork from the cabinet, she plops down on a chair and sighs exhaustedly.

"Long day?" Jackson asks.

"Yeah, kind of. I met with my lawyer and filed for

divorce!" she says excitedly. Jackson takes a step back.

"Really?" he asks, monitoring his exuberance. "That's wonderful. What made you make that decision?"

"You made a pretty strong case, didn't you?"

"Yes, I did, but I didn't think you were going to listen."

"Your boyfriend is a pretty smart man," Aurora says to me. It's the first thing she has said to me since she came in.

"I tend to think so," I say, forcing a smile.

"But you know how it is, it wasn't just that. I just came to the conclusion that I shouldn't be treated like crap anymore."

Jackson walks over and gives her a hug. I clench my jaw as I watch their embrace.

"Thanks for supporting me on this," Aurora says after they pull away.

"You can stay here for as long as you want," Jackson says. My eyes grow big and my mouth practically drops open. How the hell can he say that without running it by me first?

As much as I don't think it's a good idea for her to stay with an abusive man who hits her and makes her feel like crap, I am also not particularly keen on her staying here. Besides, it's not like she doesn't have anywhere to go.

She wrote Jackson a check for two million dollars, so she can easily afford a hotel room.

"I know and appreciate it. But I don't want to be in the way. You and Harley need your alone time."

I nod, pleasantly surprised.

"So, where are you going to go? The Ritz?"

She shrugs and looks away.

"C'mon, Aurora. You have to tell me."

She doesn't respond.

"You really don't want me to know?" Jackson asks.

"I don't mind, but I don't think you'll approve," she says after a moment. "I'm going to stay with Elliot."

"What?" Jackson hisses.

"See, told ya."

Who's Elliot? I wonder to myself. And why would Jackson care?

"Elliot and I have gotten really close recently. And I feel comfortable with him."

"You can't be serious," Jackson says.

"Who's Elliot?" I finally ask.

"Elliot Woodward. I think you met him," she says.

My body physically recoils at the sound of his name.

"Yes, she did. And he made a move on her and really disrespected her," Jackson adds.

"Listen, I know that you have your own issues with him, but I'm my own person. I make my own decisions."

"He's an asshole who is no better than your husband."

"Let me make that decision," Aurora says sternly. But Jackson doesn't let up.

"He's dangerous, Aurora. He's going to hurt you."

"Listen, I've had enough with this, okay? I'm a grown woman and I don't need your fucking input about my love life. You're my ex-husband. It's a courtesy that I'm telling you anything at all."

"A courtesy? You come crying to me every time some dick punches you in your face. Don't you know that men aren't supposed to treat you like that? I never did."

"Fuck you," Aurora says and runs to her room. She slams the door behind her, leaving us alone in the kitchen.

I reach for Jackson's hand but he just pushes me away. Fuming, he paces around the place like an animal in a small cage.

"She can't move in with that guy. We have to stop her."

"She's an adult, Jackson. She'll do what she wants."

"She has no idea what she wants."

Something suddenly starts to bother me about his reaction to her decision. Is he really just concerned about her? Or is there something different going on? I know that they have a long history together, but you'd think that after everything that she has done to him, he wouldn't give her another thought. And yet, here he is, going out of his way to help her make better choices.

"Jackson, you know that she has the right to date whoever she wants."

"Fuck that."

"I mean, I also think that Elliot Woodward is total scum, but so what? What say do we have in their relationship?"

Before he can answer me, Aurora comes out of her room rolling two bags behind her. Her eyes are shielded by sunglasses even though we are inside and it's getting dark outside. She walks right past Jackson without saying a word. He grabs her arm.

"Let go of me." She pulls away from him.

"Please, don't do this," he pleads.

"I thought I could stay and talk to you as a friend, Jackson. But I guess we're not really friends after all."

"I am your friend," Jackson pleads. "That's why I'm so concerned about you. Elliot isn't a good person, Aurora. He's going to hurt you."

She shakes her head.

"We'll just have to agree to disagree," she says and turns to me. "It was nice to meet you, Harley. Good luck...with everything."

"You, too," I mumble.

JACKSON

WHEN PROMISES ARE MADE...

A week later, we attend Harley's parents' wedding in Central Park. As my gift to them, I paid for a wedding planner who made all the arrangements and for the wedding itself. The wedding is quaint and cozy and perfect for the two of them.

Even though the wedding is small and Harley and I are the only guests, they just went to the Justice of the Peace their first time around, and Leslie requested something a bit more formal this time. The wedding coordinator does a good job creating a beautiful arbor. As we wait under the arch made of branches and vines and intertwined with wildflowers, I glance over at Harold. Dressed in a beautiful tailored tuxedo, Harold looks put together and confident but I can see that he is nervous that he is practically shaking.

"It's going to be okay," I say. "As soon as you see her walking...everything will fall into place."

I speak as if I know what I'm talking about, but my words put him at ease. He takes a deep breath and nods.

When the wedding coordinator cues them, the group of guitar players start to play the wedding march in a quiet romantic way. A few moments later, Harley appears at the end of the aisle. She is dressed in a long gown and a matching faux fur coat. Despite the coordinator's insistence, she refused to wear something made of animal fur. But this one looks just as soft and comfortable as any real version.

Harley walks slowly with her hair moving up and down with each step. She is not comfortable in those heels, but the few missteps that do happen don't seem to faze her at all. Instead, she just smiles wider and brighter.

Ever since Harold and Leslie told her about their wedding plans, Harley has been plagued by anxiety. I am glad that the wedding planning didn't take more than a week because I don't think I could've managed to support her for much longer. It's difficult to explain what it's like to try to help someone with that condition. The entire week was fraught with conflict and second-guesses. The conflict originated not so much between us but within herself. Nothing was good enough and no matter how much she tried to put the event out of her mind, she couldn't quite relax and think about anything else.

Whenever I would ask her what is bothering her so much about this, she would just shrug her shoulders, unable to put her feelings into words. Instead, most of her attention was focused on everything that took her out of her comfort zone; dress shopping, hair and makeup trial, and the fact that the bodyguard had to accompany her to all of these events.

But now? Watching her walk down the aisle, she looks effervescent. It's not just the beautiful gown or the professional hair and makeup, it's her whole being. She's glowing. The dream of every kid of divorce is coming true - her parents have fallen back in love with each other and are showing their commitment by getting re-married.

She takes her place across from me, after giving her dad a kiss on the cheek. The minister nods and the guitarists start to play a more upbeat tempo. Now, it's Leslie's turn.

She appears from behind a towering tree and walks to the end of the aisle. Dressed in a long lacy gown, this is the first dress that I have seen Leslie wear. I wouldn't be surprised if this were the first dress she has worn in years. Despite this, she looks as if she belongs in it. It's as if it were made just for her.

As she moves closer to us, I watch the way her hair frames her face with waves that are reminiscent of Harley's. A small tiara sits atop her head, holding her veil in place.

I glance over at Harold. Whatever jitters he must've felt seem to vanish. Instead, he loses himself entirely in Leslie, brushing tears out of his eyes with the back of his hand.

When she gets to the front, he leans over and lifts her veil.

"You look so...beautiful," he mumbles. Fighting tears as well, she nods and looks away for a moment.

The ceremony begins and the minister tells us that they have prepared their own vows. As I listen, I stare at Harley. Her gaze meets mine.

"I love you," I mouth to Harley. She licks her lips and mouths, "I love you, too."

I run my fingers down my thigh until I feel the little secret that I have hidden there. I don't put my hands in my pockets, I just feel the outside of it. I trace the outline of the little circle until I reach the rock. My heart skips a beat. The ring is light, but it also feels like it weighs five hundred pounds. I bought it a long time ago, the day after we first spent a night together. It was too soon to propose, so I kept it safe this whole time until the regrets started to pile up.

I didn't propose earlier because it was too soon. Not according to me, or my heart, but it felt too soon in our relationship and I didn't want to hear no. But then when she was taken from me, the fact that I waited to ask for her hand in marriage tore me up inside. I realized that I loved her and I bought this ring to show her how much I loved her. So, why did I wait? What was I waiting for?

"I now pronounce you husband and wife," the minister says to Leslie and Harold. "You may now kiss."

When I run my finger along the outline of her engagement ring, a smile comes over my face and a feeling of utter contentment fills my soul.

"I love you," I whisper when I take Harley's hand and lead her down the aisle after the newlyweds.

* * *

THANK you for reading Tangled up in Lace!

I hope you are enjoying Harley and Jackson's story. Can't wait to find out what happens next?

One-click Tangled up in Hate Now!

Epic love requires an epic sacrifice...

A long time ago, I borrowed money from a very powerful family. I paid my debt, but they have come for more.

They want everything that I have built and they will hurt her if I refuse.

Harley doesn't understand why I have to break her heart. She hates me, but at least she's okay...for now.

But what happens when sending her away isn't enough?

What happens when I lose everything?

One-click Tangled up in Hate now!

SIGN up for my **newsletter** to find out when I have new books!

You can also join my Facebook group, **Charlotte**

Byrd's Reader Club, for exclusive giveaways and sneak peaks of future books.

I appreciate you sharing my books and telling your friends about them. Reviews help readers find my books! Please leave a review on your favorite site.

BLACK EDGE

Want to read a "Decadent, delicious, & dangerously addictive!" romance you will not be able to put down? The entire series is out! **1-Click Black Edge NOW!**

I don't belong here.

I'm in way over my head. But I have debts to pay.

They call my name. The spotlight is on. The auction starts.

Mr. Black is the highest bidder. He's dark, rich, and powerful. He likes to play games.

The only rule is there are no rules.

But it's just one night. **What's the worst that can happen?**

1-Click BLACK EDGE Now!

START READING BLACK EDGE ON THE NEXT PAGE!

CHAPTER 1- ELLIE

WHEN THE INVITATION ARRIVES...

"Here it is! Here it is!" my roommate Caroline yells at the top of her lungs as she runs into my room.

We were friends all through Yale and we moved to New York together after graduation.

Even though I've known Caroline for what feels like a million years, I am still shocked by the exuberance of her voice. It's quite loud given the smallness of her body.

Caroline is one of those super skinny girls who can eat pretty much anything without gaining a pound.

Unfortunately, I am not that talented. In fact, my body seems to have the opposite gift. I can eat nothing but vegetables for a week straight, eat one slice of pizza, and gain a pound.

"What is it?" I ask, forcing myself to sit up.

It's noon and I'm still in bed.

My mother thinks I'm depressed and wants me to see her shrink.

She might be right, but I can't fathom the strength.

"The invitation!" Caroline says jumping in bed next to me.

I stare at her blankly.

And then suddenly it hits me.

This must be *the* invitation.

"You mean...it's..."

"Yes!" she screams and hugs me with excitement.

"Oh my God!" She gasps for air and pulls away from me almost as quickly.

"Hey, you know I didn't brush my teeth yet," I say turning my face away from hers.

"Well, what are you waiting for? Go brush them," she instructs.

Begrudgingly, I make my way to the bathroom.

We have been waiting for this invitation for some time now.

And by we, I mean Caroline.

I've just been playing along, pretending to care, not really expecting it to show up.

Without being able to contain her excitement, Caroline bursts through the door when my mouth is still full of toothpaste.

She's jumping up and down, holding a box in her hand.

"Wait, what's that?" I mumble and wash my mouth out with water.

"This is it!" Caroline screeches and pulls me into the living room before I have a chance to wipe my mouth with a towel.

"But it's a box," I say staring at her.

"Okay, okay," Caroline takes a couple of deep yoga breaths, exhaling loudly.

She puts the box carefully on our dining room table. There's no address on it.

It looks something like a fancy gift box with a big monogrammed C in the middle.

Is the C for Caroline?

"Is this how it came? There's no address on it?" I ask.

"It was hand-delivered," Caroline whispers.

I hold my breath as she carefully removes the top part, revealing the satin and silk covered wood box inside.

The top of it is gold plated with whimsical twirls all around the edges, and the mirrored area is engraved with her full name.

Caroline Elizabeth Kennedy Spruce.

Underneath her name is a date, one week in the future. 8 PM.

We stare at it for a few moments until Caroline reaches for the elegant knob to open the box.

Inside, Caroline finds a custom monogram made of foil in gold on silk emblazoned on the inside of the flap cover.

There's also a folio covered in silk. Caroline carefully opens the folio and finds another foil monogram and the invitation.

The inside invitation is one layer, shimmer white, with gold writing.

"Is this for real? How many layers of invitation are there?" I ask.

But the presentation is definitely doing its job. We are both duly impressed.

"There's another knob," I say, pointing to the knob in front of the box.

I'm not sure how we had missed it before.

Caroline carefully pulls on this knob, revealing a drawer that holds the inserts (a card with directions and a response card).

"Oh my God, I can't go to this alone," Caroline mumbles, turning to me.

I stare blankly at her.

Getting invited to this party has been her dream ever since she found out about it from someone in the Cicada 17, a super-secret society at Yale.

"Look, here, it says that I can bring a friend," she yells out even though I'm standing right next to her.

"It probably says a date. A plus one?" I say.

"No, a friend. Girl preferred," Caroline reads off the invitation card.

That part of the invitation is in very small ink, as if someone made the person stick it on, without their express permission.

"I don't want to crash," I say.

Frankly, I don't really want to go.

These kind of upper-class events always make me feel a little bit uncomfortable.

"Hey, aren't you supposed to be at work?" I ask.

"Eh, I took a day off," Caroline says waving her arm. "I knew that the invitation would come today and I just couldn't deal with work. You know how it is."

I nod. Sort of.

Caroline and I seem like we come from the same world.

We both graduated from private school, we both went to Yale, and our parents belong to the same exclusive country club in Greenwich, Connecticut.

But we're not really that alike.

Caroline's family has had money for many generations going back to the railroads.

My parents were an average middle class family from Connecticut.

They were both teachers and our idea of summering was renting a 1-bedroom bungalow near Clearwater, FL for a week.

But then my parents got divorced when I was 8, and my mother started tutoring kids to make extra money.

The pay was the best in Greenwich, where parents paid more than $100 an hour.

And that's how she met, Mitch Willoughby, my stepfather.

He was a widower with a five-year old daughter who was not doing well after her mom's untimely death.

Even though Mom didn't usually tutor anyone younger than 12, she agreed to take a meeting with Mitch and his daughter because $200 an hour was too much to turn down.

Three months later, they were in love and six

months later, he asked her to marry him on top of the Eiffel Tower.

They got married, when I was 11, in a huge 450-person ceremony in Nantucket.

So even though Caroline and I run in the same circles, we're not really from the same circle.

It has nothing to do with her, she's totally accepting, it's me.

I don't always feel like I belong.

Caroline majored in art-history at Yale, and she now works at an exclusive contemporary art gallery in Soho.

It's chic and tiny, featuring only 3 pieces of art at a time.

Ash, the owner - I'm not sure if that's her first or last name - mainly keeps the space as a showcase. What the gallery really specializes in is going to wealthy people's homes and choosing their art for them.

They're basically interior designers, but only for art.

None of the pieces sell for anything less than $200 grand, but Caroline's take home salary is about $21,000.

Clearly, not enough to pay for our 2 bedroom apartment in Chelsea.

Her parents cover her part of the rent and pay all of her other expenses.

Mine do too, of course.

Well, Mitch does.

I only make about $27,000 at my writer's assistant job and that's obviously not covering my half of our $6,000 per month apartment.

So, what's the difference between me and Caroline?

I guess the only difference is that I feel bad about taking the money.

I have a $150,000 school loan from Yale that I don't want Mitch to pay for.

It's my loan and I'm going to pay for it myself, dammit.

Plus, unlike Caroline, I know that real people don't really live like this.

Real people like my dad, who is being pressured to sell the house for more than a million dollars that he and my mom bought back in the late 80's (the neighborhood has gone up in price and teachers now have to make way for tech entrepreneurs and real estate moguls).

"How can you just not go to work like that? Didn't you use all of your sick days flying to Costa Rica last month?" I ask.

"Eh, who cares? Ash totally understands. Besides, she totally owes me. If it weren't for me, she would've never closed that geek millionaire who had the hots for me and ended up buying close to a million dollars' worth of art for his new mansion."

Caroline does have a way with men.

She's fun and outgoing and perky.

The trick, she once told me, is to figure out exactly what the guy wants to hear.

Because a geek millionaire, as she calls anyone who has made money in tech, does not want to hear the same thing that a football player wants to hear.

And neither of them want to hear what a trust fund playboy wants to hear.

But Caroline isn't a gold digger.

Not at all.

Her family owns half the East Coast.

And when it comes to men, she just likes to have fun.

I look at the time.

It's my day off, but that doesn't mean that I want to spend it in bed in my pajamas, listening to Caroline obsessing over what she's going to wear.

No, today, is my day to actually get some writing done.

I'm going to Starbucks, getting a table in the

back, near the bathroom, and am actually going to finish this short story that I've been working on for a month.

Or maybe start a new one.

I go to my room and start getting dressed.

I have to wear something comfortable, but something that's not exactly work clothes.

I hate how all of my clothes have suddenly become work clothes. It's like they've been tainted.

They remind me of work and I can't wear them out anymore on any other occasion. I'm not a big fan of my work, if you can't tell.

Caroline follows me into my room and plops down on my bed.

I take off my pajamas and pull on a pair of leggings.

Ever since these have become the trend, I find myself struggling to force myself into a pair of jeans.

They're just so comfortable!

"Okay, I've come to a decision," Caroline says. "You *have* to come with me!"

"Oh, I have to come with you?" I ask, incredulously. "Yeah, no, I don't think so."

"Oh c'mon! Please! Pretty please! It will be so much fun!"

"Actually, you can't make any of those promises.

You have no idea what it will be," I say, putting on a long sleeve shirt and a sweater with a zipper in the front.

Layers are important during this time of year.

The leaves are changing colors, winds are picking up, and you never know if it's going to be one of those gorgeous warm, crisp New York days they like to feature in all those romantic comedies or a soggy, overcast dreary day that only shows up in one scene at the end when the two main characters fight or break up (but before they get back together again).

"Okay, yes, I see your point," Caroline says, sitting up and crossing her legs. "But here is what we *do* know. We do know that it's going to be amazing. I mean, look at the invitation. It's a freakin' box with engravings and everything!"

Usually, Caroline is much more eloquent and better at expressing herself.

"Okay, yes, the invitation is impressive," I admit.

"And as you know, the invitation is everything. I mean, it really sets the mood for the party. The event! And not just the mood. It establishes a certain expectation. And this box..."

"Yes, the invitation definitely sets up a certain expectation," I agree.

"So?"

"So?" I ask her back.

"Don't you want to find out what that expectation is?"

"No." I shake my head categorically.

"Okay. So what else do we know?" Caroline asks rhetorically as I pack away my Mac into my bag.

"I have to go, Caroline," I say.

"No, listen. The yacht. Of course, the yacht. How could I bury the lead like that?" She jumps up and down with excitement again.

"We also know that it's going to be this super exclusive event on a *yacht*! And not just some small 100 footer, but a *mega*-yacht."

I stare at her blankly, pretending to not be impressed.

When Caroline first found out about this party, through her ex-boyfriend, we spent days trying to figure out what made this event so special.

But given that neither of us have been on a yacht before, at least not a mega-yacht – we couldn't quite get it.

"You know the yacht is going to be amazing!"

"Yes, of course," I give in. "But that's why I'm sure that you're going to have a wonderful time by yourself. I have to go."

I grab my keys and toss them into the bag.

"Ellie," Caroline says.

The tone of her voice suddenly gets very serious, to match the grave expression on her face.

"Ellie, please. I don't think I can go by myself."

CHAPTER 2 - ELLIE

WHEN YOU HAVE COFFEE WITH A GUY YOU CAN'T HAVE...

And that's pretty much how I was roped into going.

You don't know Caroline, but if you did, the first thing you'd find out is that she is not one to take things seriously.

Nothing fazes her.

Nothing worries her.

Sometimes she is the most enlightened person on earth, other times she's the densest.

Most of the time, I'm jealous of the fact that she simply lives life in the present.

"So, you're going?" my friend Tom asks.

He brought me my pumpkin spice latte, the first one of the season!

I close my eyes and inhale it's sweet aroma before taking the first sip.

But even before its wonderful taste of cinnamon and nutmeg runs down my throat, Tom is already criticizing my decision.

"I can't believe you're actually going," he says.

"Oh my God, now I know it's officially fall," I change the subject.

"Was there actually such a thing as autumn before the pumpkin spice latte? I mean, I remember that we had falling leaves, changing colors, all that jazz, but without this...it's like Christmas without a Christmas tree."

"Ellie, it's a day after Labor Day," Tom rolls his eyes. "It's not fall yet."

I take another sip. "Oh yes, I do believe it is."

"Stop changing the subject," Tom takes a sip of his plain black coffee.

How he doesn't get bored with that thing, I'll never know.

But that's the thing about Tom.

He's reliable.

Always on time, never late.

It's nice. That's what I have always liked about him.

He's basically the opposite of Caroline in every way.

And that's what makes seeing him like this, as only a friend, so hard.

"Why are you going there? Can't Caroline go by herself?" Tom asks, looking straight into my eyes.

His hair has this annoying tendency of falling into his face just as he's making a point – as a way of accentuating it.

It's actually quite vexing especially given how irresistible it makes him look.

His eyes twinkle under the low light in the back of the Starbucks.

"I'm going as her plus one," I announce.

I make my voice extra perky on purpose.

So that it portrays excitement, rather than apprehensiveness, which is actually how I'm feeling over the whole thing.

"She's making you go as her plus one," Tom announces as a matter a fact. He knows me too well.

"I just don't get it, Ellie. I mean, why bother? It's a super yacht filled with filthy rich people. I mean, how fun can that party be?"

"Jealous much?" I ask.

"I'm not jealous at all!" He jumps back in his seat. "If that's what you think..."

He lets his words trail off and suddenly the conversation takes on a more serious mood.

"You don't have to worry, I'm not going to miss your engagement party," I say quietly. It's the weekend after I get back."

He shakes his head and insists that that's not what he's worried about.

"I just don't get it Ellie," he says.

You don't get it?

You don't get why I'm going?

I've had feelings for you for, what, two years now?

But the time was never right.

At first, I was with my boyfriend and the night of our breakup, you decided to kiss me.

You totally caught me off guard.

And after that long painful breakup, I wasn't ready for a relationship.

And you, my best friend, you weren't really a rebound contender.

And then, just as I was about to tell you how I felt, you spend the night with Carrie.

Beautiful, wealthy, witty Carrie. Carrie Warrenhouse, the current editor of BuzzPost, the online magazine where we both work, and the daughter of Edward Warrenhouse, the owner of BuzzPost.

Oh yeah, and on top of all that, you also started seeing her and then asked her to marry you.

And now you two are getting married on Valentine's Day.

And I'm really happy for you.

Really.

Truly.

The only problem is that I'm also in love with you.

And now, I don't know what the hell to do with all of this except get away from New York.

Even if it's just for a few days.

But of course, I can't say any of these things.

Especially the last part.

"This hasn't been the best summer," I say after a few moments. "And I just want to do something fun. Get out of town. Go to a party. Because that's all this is, a party."

"That's not what I heard," Tom says.

"What do you mean?"

"Ever since you told me you were going, I started looking into this event.

And the rumor is that it's not what it is."

I shake my head, roll my eyes.

"What? You don't believe me?" Tom asks incredulously.

I shake my head.

"Okay, what? What did you hear?"

"It's basically like a Playboy Mansion party on steroids. It's totally out of control. Like one big orgy."

"And you would know what a Playboy Mansion party is like," I joke.

"I'm being serious, Ellie. I'm not sure this is a good place for you. I mean, you're not Caroline."

"And what the hell does that mean?" I ask.

Now, I'm actually insulted.

At first, I was just listening because I thought he was being protective.

But now...

"What you don't think I'm fun enough? You don't think I like to have a good time?" I ask.

"That's not what I meant," Tom backtracks. I start to gather my stuff. "What are you doing?"

"No, you know what," I stop packing up my stuff. "I'm not leaving. You're leaving."

"Why?"

"Because I came here to write. I have work to do. I staked out this table and I'm not leaving until I have something written. I thought you wanted to have coffee with me. I thought we were friends. I didn't realize that you came here to chastise me about my decisions."

"That's not what I'm doing," Tom says, without getting out of his chair.

"You have to leave Tom. I want you to leave."

"I just don't understand what happened to us," he says getting up, reluctantly.

I stare at him as if he has lost his mind.

"You have no right to tell me what I can or can't do. You don't even have the right to tell your fiancée. Unless you don't want her to stay your fiancée for long."

"I'm not trying to tell you what to do, Ellie. I'm just worried. This super exclusive party on some mega-yacht, that's not you. That's not us."

"Not us? You've got to be kidding," I shake my head. "You graduated from Princeton, Tom. Your father is an attorney at one of the most prestigious law-firms in Boston. He has argued cases before the Supreme Court. You're going to marry the heir to the Warrenhouse fortune. I'm so sick and tired of your working class hero attitude, I can't even tell you. Now, are you going to leave or should I?"

The disappointment that I saw in Tom's eyes hurt me to my very soul.

But he had hurt me.

His engagement came completely out of left field.

I had asked him to give me some time after my breakup and after waiting for only two months, he started dating Carrie.

And then they moved in together. And then he asked her to marry him.

And throughout all that, he just sort of pretended that we were still friends.

Just like none of this ever happened.

I open my computer and stare at the half written story before me.

Earlier today, before Caroline, before Tom, I had all of these ideas.

I just couldn't wait to get started.

But now...I doubted that I could even spell my name right.

Staring at a non-moving blinker never fuels the writing juices.

I close my computer and look around the place.

All around me, people are laughing and talking.

Leggings and Uggs are back in season – even though the days are still warm and crispy.

It hasn't rained in close to a week and everyone's

good mood seems to be energized by the bright rays of the afternoon sun.

Last spring, I was certain that Tom and I would get together over the summer and I would spend the fall falling in love with my best friend.

And now?

Now, he's engaged to someone else.

Not just someone else – my boss!

And we just had a fight over some stupid party that I don't even really want to go to.

He's right, of course.

It's not my style.

My family might have money, but that's not the world in which I'm comfortable.

I'm always standing on the sidelines and it's not going to be any different at this party.

But if I don't go now, after this, that means that I'm listening to him.

And he has no right to tell me what to do.

So, I have to go.

How did everything get so messed up?

CHAPTER 3 - ELLIE

WHEN YOU GO SHOPPING FOR THE PARTY OF A LIFETIME...

"What the hell are you still doing hanging out with that asshole?" Caroline asks dismissively.

We are in Elle's, a small boutique in Soho, where you can shop by appointment only.

I didn't even know these places existed until Caroline introduced me to the concept.

Caroline is not a fan of Tom.

They never got along, not since he called her an East Side snob at our junior year Christmas party at Yale and she called him a middle class poseur.

Neither insult was very creative, but their insults got better over the years as their hatred for each other grew.

You know how in the movies, two characters who

hate each other in the beginning always end up falling in love by the end?

Well, for a while, I actually thought that would happen to them.

If not fall in love, at least hook up. But no, they stayed steadfast in their hatred.

"That guy is such a tool. I mean, who the hell is he to tell you what to do anyway? It's not like you're his girlfriend," Caroline says placing a silver beaded bandage dress to her body and extending her right leg in front.

Caroline is definitely a knock out.

She's 5'10", 125 pounds with legs that go up to her chin.

In fact, from far away, she seems to be all blonde hair and legs and nothing else.

"I think he was just concerned, given all the stuff that is out there about this party."

"Okay, first of all, you have to stop calling it a party."

"Why? What is it?"

"It's not a party. It's like calling a wedding a party. Is it a party? Yes. But is it bigger than that."

"I had no idea that you were so sensitive to language. Fine. What do you want me to call it?'

"An experience," she announces, completely seriously.

"Are you kidding me? No way. There's no way I'm going to call it an experience."

We browse in silence for a few moments.

Some of the dresses and tops and shoes are pretty, some aren't.

I'm the first to admit that I do not have the vocabulary or knowledge to appreciate a place like this.

Now, Caroline on the other hand...

"Oh my God, I'm just in love with all these one of a kind pieces you have here," she says to the woman upfront who immediately starts to beam with pride.

"That's what we're going for."

"These statement bags and the detailing on these booties – agh! To die for, right?" Caroline says and they both turn to me.

"Yeah, totally," I agree blindly.

"And these high-end core pieces, I could just wear this every day!" Caroline pulls up a rather structured cream colored short sleeve shirt with a tassel hem and a boxy fit.

I'm not sure what makes that shirt a so-called core piece, but I go with the flow.

I'm out of my element and I know it.

"Okay, so what are we supposed to wear to this *experience* if we don't even know what's going to be going on there."

"I'm not exactly sure but definitely not jeans and t-shirts," Caroline says referring to my staple outfit. "But the invitation also said not to worry. They have all the necessities if we forget something."

As I continue to aimlessly browse, my mind starts to wander.

And goes back to Tom.

I met Tom at the Harvard-Yale game.

He was my roommate's boyfriend's high school best friend and he came up for the weekend to visit him.

We became friends immediately.

One smile from him, even on Skype, made all of my worries disappear.

He just sort of got me, the way no one really did.

After graduation, we applied to work a million different online magazines and news outlets, but BuzzPost was the one place that took both of us.

We didn't exactly plan to end up at the same place, but it was a nice coincidence.

He even asked if I wanted to be his roommate – but I had already agreed to room with Caroline.

He ended up in this crappy fourth floor walkup

in Hell's Kitchen – one of the only buildings that they haven't gentrified yet.

So, the rent was still somewhat affordable. Like I said, Tom likes to think of himself as a working class hero even though his upbringing is far from it.

Whenever he came over to our place, he always made fun of how expensive the place was, but it was always in good fun.

At least, it felt like it at the time.

Now?

I'm not so sure anymore.

"Do you think that Tom is really going to get married?" I ask Caroline while we're changing.

She swings my curtain open in front of the whole store.

I'm topless, but luckily I'm facing away from her and the assistant is buried in her phone.

"What are you doing?" I shriek and pull the curtain closed.

"What are you thinking?" she demands.

I manage to grab a shirt and cover myself before Caroline pulls the curtain open again.

She is standing before me in only a bra and a matching pair of panties – completely confident and unapologetic.

I think she's my spirit animal.

"Who cares about Tom?" Caroline demands.

"I do," I say meekly.

"Well, you shouldn't. He's a dick. You are way too good for him. I don't even understand what you see in him."

"He's my friend," I say as if that explains everything.

Caroline knows how long I've been in love with Tom.

She knows everything.

At times, I wish I hadn't been so open.

But other times, it's nice to have someone to talk to.

Even if she isn't exactly understanding.

"You can't just go around pining for him, Ellie. You can do so much better than him. You were with your ex and he just hung around waiting and waiting. Never telling you how he felt. Never making any grand gestures."

Caroline is big on gestures.

The grander the better.

She watches a lot of movies and she demands them of her dates.

And the funny thing is that you often get exactly what you ask from the world.

"I don't care about that," I say. "We were in the wrong place for each other.

I was with someone and then I wasn't ready to jump into another relationship right away.

And then...he and Carrie got together."

"There's no such thing as not the right time. Life is what you make it, Ellie. You're in control of your life. And I hate the fact that you're acting like you're not the main character in your own movie."

"I don't even know what you're talking about," I say.

"All I'm saying is that you deserve someone who tells you how he feels. Someone who isn't afraid of rejection. Someone who isn't afraid to put it all out there."

"Maybe that's who you want," I say.

"And that's not who you want?" Caroline says taking a step back away from me.

I think about it for a moment.

"Well, no I wouldn't say that. It is who I want," I finally say. "But I had a boyfriend then. And Tom and I were friends. So I couldn't expect him to—"

"You couldn't expect him to put it all out there? Tell you how he feels and take the risk of getting hurt?" Caroline cuts me off.

I hate to admit it, but that's exactly what I want.

That's exactly what I wanted from him back then.

I didn't want him to just hang around being my friend, making me question my feelings for him.

And if he had done that, if he had told me how he felt about me earlier, before my awful breakup, then I would've jumped in.

I would've broken up with my ex immediately to be with him.

"So, is that what I should do now? Now that things are sort of reversed?" I ask.

"What do you mean?"

"I mean, now that he's the one in the relationship. Should I just put it all out there? Tell him how I feel. Leave it all on the table, so to speak."

Caroline takes a moment to think about this.

I appreciate it because I know how little she thinks of him.

"Because I don't know if I can," I add quietly.

"Maybe that's your answer right there," Caroline finally says. "If you did want him, really want him to be yours, then you wouldn't be able to not to. You'd have to tell him."

I go back into my dressing room and pull the curtain closed.

I look at myself in the mirror.

The pale girl with green eyes and long dark hair is a coward.

She is afraid of life.

Afraid to really live.

Would this ever change?

CHAPTER 4 - ELLIE

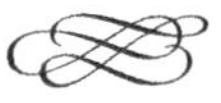

WHEN YOU DECIDE TO LIVE YOUR LIFE...

"Are you ready?" Caroline bursts into my room. "Our cab is downstairs."

No, I'm not ready.

Not at all.

But I'm going.

I take one last look in the mirror and grab my suitcase.

As the cab driver loads our bags into the trunk, Caroline takes my hand, giddy with excitement.

Excited is not how I would describe my state of being.

More like reluctant.

And terrified.

When I get into the cab, my stomach drops and I feel like I'm going to throw up.

But then the feeling passes.

"I can't believe this is actually happening," I say.

"I know, right? I'm so happy you're doing this with me, Ellie. I mean, really. I don't know if I could go by myself."

After ten minutes of meandering through the convoluted streets of lower Manhattan, the cab drops us off in front of a nondescript office building.

"Is the party here?" I ask.

Caroline shakes her head with a little smile on her face.

She knows something I don't know.

I can tell by that mischievous look on her face.

"What's going on?" I ask.

But she doesn't give in.

Instead, she just nudges me inside toward the security guard at the front desk.

She hands him a card, he nods, and shows us to the elevator.

"Top floor," he says.

When we reach the top floor, the elevator doors swing open on the roof and a strong gust of wind knocks into me.

Out of the corner of my eye, I see it.

The helicopter.

The blades are already going.

A man approaches us and takes our bags.

"What are we doing here?" I yell on top of my lungs.

But Caroline doesn't hear me.

I follow her inside the helicopter, ducking my head to make sure that I get in all in one piece.

A few minutes later, we take off.

We fly high above Manhattan, maneuvering past the buildings as if we're birds.

I've never been in a helicopter before and, a part of me, wishes that I'd had some time to process this beforehand.

"I didn't tell you because I thought you would freak," Caroline says into her headset.

She knows me too well.

She pulls out her phone and we pose for a few selfies.

"It's beautiful up here," I say looking out the window.

In the afternoon sun, the Manhattan skyline is breathtaking.

The yellowish red glow bounces off the glass buildings and shimmers in the twilight.

I don't know where we are going, but for the first time in a long time, I don't care.

I stay in the moment and enjoy it for everything it's worth.

Quickly the skyscrapers and the endless parade of bridges disappear and all that remains below us is the glistening of the deep blue sea.

And then suddenly, somewhere in the distance I see it.

The yacht.

At first, it appears as barely a speck on the horizon.

But as we fly closer, it grows in size.

By the time we land, it seems to be the size of its own island.

* * *

A TALL, beautiful woman waves to us as we get off the helicopter.

She's holding a plate with glasses of champagne and nods to a man in a tuxedo next to her to take our bags.

"Wow, that was quite an entrance," Caroline says to me.

"Mr. Black knows how to welcome his guests,"

the woman says. "My name is Lizbeth and I am here to serve you."

Lizbeth shows us around the yacht and to our stateroom.

"There will be cocktails right outside when you're ready," Lizbeth said before leaving us alone.

As soon as she left, we grabbed hands and let out a big yelp.

"Oh my God! Can you believe this place?" Caroline asks.

"No, it's amazing," I say, running over to the balcony. The blueness of the ocean stretched out as far as the eye could see.

"Are you going to change for cocktails?" Caroline asks, sitting down at the vanity. "The helicopter did a number on my hair."

We both crack up laughing.

Neither of us have ever been on a helicopter before – let alone a boat this big.

I decide against a change of clothes – my Nordstrom leggings and polka dot blouse should do just fine for cocktail hour.

But I do slip off my pair of flats and put on a nice pair of pumps, to dress up the outfit a little bit.

While Caroline changes into her short black

dress, I brush the tangles out of my hair and reapply my lipstick.

"Ready?" Caroline asks.

Can't wait to read more? **One-Click BLACK EDGE Now!**

ABOUT CHARLOTTE BYRD

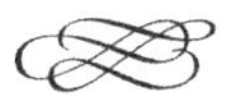

Charlotte Byrd is the bestselling author of many contemporary romance novels. She lives in Southern California with her husband, son, and a crazy toy Australian Shepherd. She loves books, hot weather and crystal blue waters.

Write her here:

charlotte@charlotte-byrd.com

Check out her books here:

www.charlotte-byrd.com

Connect with her here:

www.facebook.com/charlottebyrdbooks

Instagram: @charlottebyrdbooks

Twitter: @ByrdAuthor

Facebook Group: Charlotte Byrd's Reader Club

Newsletter

Made in the USA
Las Vegas, NV
25 May 2024